DEATH KOMETH

Death Kometh

GARY HAYWOOD

Map

SHADOOW EVIRY
MISTRAL that DEVOURS NAMES
IROSTWILDS
MURMURS of the BLACK WISTER
JUENMIALE
CONVERGENCE
THUNDER FLAKS
WHNDGROSS FLAIHS
STUNDERWEEKS
SIROCCO of the FORSAKEN DRAFT
ZEPHYR the SHATTERED BREATH
ASHEN WASTE

Clan Glyphs'

Weapons

WEAPONS OF THE WIND CLANS

MURMURS OF THE BLACK
WISPER

MISTRAL THAT DEVOURS
NAMES

WHISPERBLADES   THE CRESCENT
PAIR

NAMEKEEPER   FROSTLANCE

ZEPHYR THE SHATTERED
BREATH

SIROCCO OF THE
FORSAKEN DRAFT

FLICKERBLADES   ZEPHYR KNIVES

THUNDERBRAND   BOLTCLEAVER

THE SHATTERED TEMPEST

BLAZEWAKE GREATSWORD   THUNDERBRAND

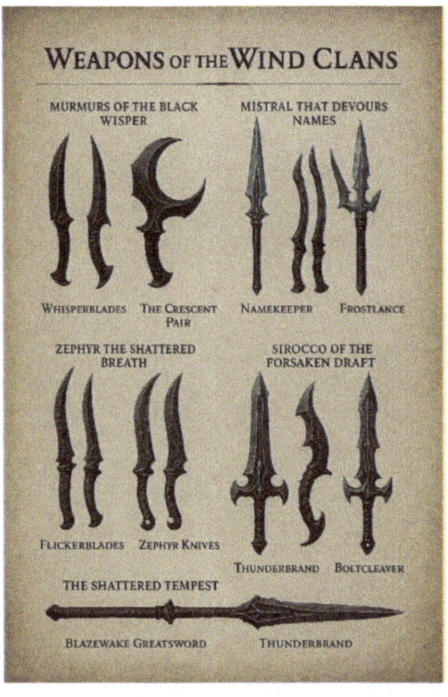

Introduction

A storm is waking... and humanity has no idea it already lost.

Death Kometh drops you into a world where the winds themselves choose sides, where ancient forces rise through the cracks of history, and where death isn't an ending—it's a command. Five clans once shaped by honor now bleed under a power older than myth. Their warriors don't fight for territory or royalty... they fight the invisible.

This isn't a classic fantasy tale. It's a war built from hunger, silence, and ancient betrayal. Battles don't just happen in the shadows—they happen inside the wind that surrounds you every moment of your life.

At the center stands a solitary figure—created by the storm, feared by all clans, and bound to a destiny he never asked for. The world expects him to save them. The wind intends to break him.

If you're ready for a story that blends mythic warfare, assassin-style combat, elemental horror, and a universe where nature itself decides who lives... and who disappears—step into Kometh.

Because death isn't coming.

Death is already here.

1st Book

Present Day

P^{art} I

R ecorded in the Season of the Fractured Winds
The winds were never meant to choose sides.

Long before clans carved scars into the world, before storms learned to taste blood, before names themselves could be devoured, the winds moved freely — wild, eternal, untouched by human hands. But the moment man listened too closely, the winds began to whisper. And those whispers changed everything.

Five winds broke away from the natural world. Five breaths gained form. Five tempests learned hunger. These winds found warriors — or perhaps they created them — shaping each clan into a reflection of their nature: silent, erasing, shattered, forsaken, and stormborn.

This book does not glorify their power.
It warns of what happens when the wind remembers you.

What follows is not myth.
Not rumor.
Not legend passed through trembling voices.

These are the chronicles sealed in stone, bone, and storm — the firsthand accounts of those who walked beneath winds that could kill, awaken, or erase entire histories.

The clans call this age The Gathering of Kometh.

The rest of the world simply calls it the beginning of the end.

From the Codex of Broken Winds
When the sky cracked for the first time, the world mistook it for thunder. Only the clans understood what had truly happened: a new wind had arrived — one that did not belong to this world.

A death-wind.

Its coming stirred every forgotten myth, every buried alliance, every fracture that once tore the five clans apart. Old grudges woke like sleeping serpents. Sealed wars began to whisper again. And somewhere, beneath a monolith built to trap an impossible storm, something ancient started to breathe.

That is why this chronicle exists.

To understand the present, one must begin with the origins of the winds — with the silent chasms that birthed the Black Wisper, the blizzard that stole identities to create the Mistral, the divine breath that shattered and became Zephyr, the forsaken desert draft that saved the unwanted, and the celestial storm that broke itself into the Tempest.

Each clan carries the burden of its creation.
Each inherits a curse written into its wind.

Their stories do not run parallel — they collide, fracture, and cut through each other like shifting currents. No single clan is innocent. None are righteous. All are necessary.

Because the wind that Kometh does not destroy only the weak.
It destroys the unprepared.

This book begins at the moment all five winds twist toward the same horizon. A moment when assassins move in silence, names vanish from memory, warriors flicker through shattered breaths, desert blades scorch the earth, and stormborn champions wake from centuries of forced sleep.

Here lies the truth of the clans — not the legends whispered by cowards, but the reality carved into the bones of those who survived the first war.

T HE WIND THAT WOKE THE DEAD

The sky fractured long before anyone heard it.

A thin line of light ripped across the clouds — silent at first, then vibrating like a scream trapped inside the world's ribs. Birds fell still. Trees bent without a breeze. On the highest ridge of the Forsaken Continent, five warriors from five clans lifted their heads at the exact same moment.

They felt it.

Every clan did.

The wind... changed.

The Tempestborn was the first to move. A towering figure wrapped in storm-etched armor, he raised his hand toward the torn sky. His gauntlet crackled. The air around him spiraled in tight, violent circles.

"It's waking again," he muttered.

Far below, in the soundless caverns of the Black Wisper, candles extinguished themselves. The Unheard — a figure whose footsteps never touched the ground — paused mid-stride.

In silence, he whispered a word that never made a sound.

Above the frozen cliffs, the Nameless One of Mistral felt the tear in the world tug at the edges of memory. His followers forgot their own names for a heartbeat. He smiled.

Across the dunes, heat shimmered unnaturally as the Scorched Sovereign lifted her scorched staff — the desert wind cowering at her feet.

And in the broken forests, the Fragmented Master of Zephyr flickered into and out of existence, appearing five times in five different places before stabilizing.

The sky rippled.

The tear widened.

A gust spilled out — not air, not storm, not anything belonging to this world.

A death-wind.

It rolled through mountains and deserts and caverns without touching a single leaf, yet every warrior felt its hand grip the back of their neck.

The Tempestborn's voice carried on a thunderless breath:

"The Second Storm War has begun."

The tear finally released its sound — a low, ancient groan like the earth remembering something it swore to forget.

And beneath a monolith cracked by centuries of strain... something exhaled.

"The Whisper That Should Not Be Heard"

Clan: Murmurs of the Black Wisper

Location: The Silent Chasm

No wind ever touched the Silent Chasm.

That was the rule.

That was the curse.

Shadowling Kaelen dropped into the cavern with a rope-less descent, his movements quiet even to himself. Every recruit feared their first mission here — the chasm listened. The chasm judged. And sometimes, it answered.

He reached the bottom. Total darkness greeted him.

Kaelen exhaled.

The sound vanished.

Not muffled.

Not absorbed.

Erased.

He steadied his breath, remembering the Unheard's instructions:

If the wind speaks to you, do not reply.

If the whisper follows you, do not run.

If you hear your own voice in the dark... you are already lost.

Kaelen stepped forward, fingers brushing the cavern wall. Cold stone. Deep cracks. Something ancient pulsing beneath.

Then he heard it — faint, broken, wrong.

A whisper.

Not carried on wind.

Not produced by anything living.

A whisper without breath.

It circled him.

Behind.

Above.

Inside.

He froze.

The whisper sharpened into a fragmented phrase:

"...it wakes..."

Kaelen's heart hammered. This was not the whisper of his clan. This was older, heavier, vibrating in his ribs like a held-back scream.

Another fragment:

"...Kometh..."

He stumbled back. The whisper lunged at him — not a sound, but a force pressing against the back of his skull. His vision blurred.

Suddenly a hand touched his shoulder.

Kaelen spun, daggers out.

The Unheard stood behind him, hovering an inch above the ground. His mask reflected no light.

"You heard it," the Unheard said quietly — the only clan leader capable of making sound within the chasm.

Kaelen nodded shakily.

The Unheard turned toward the darkness.

"Then the world is changing. The winds have begun to speak a language that predates our clans."

A deep rumble traveled up through the ground.

The walls shook.

The whisper rose — louder now, layered with multiple broken voices.

"...the storm... breaks..."

The Unheard lifted his hand.

"Kaelen," he said, "run this message to the clan pacts: The death-wind has returned. None are ready."

Kaelen sprinted toward the exit.

The whisper followed him the entire way.

2   "THE SUMMIT OF FRACTURED WINDS"
Location: The Convergence Plateau

The plateau was chosen because no clan could claim it. It sat at the dead center of the continent — a place where every wind that crossed it died, as if the land itself swallowed breath.

Kaelen arrived with the Black Wisper delegation, standing behind the Unheard. No one spoke. Not yet. Not until the winds themselves settled.

Sirocco arrived next — heat shimmering around them, distorting the air. The Scorched Sovereign stood at their front, her voice like sunburn on stone.

"Let this meeting be short," she said. "The desert burns for no one."

Zephyr flickered into existence one warrior at a time.

The Fragmented Master appeared last, body glitching in and out of alignment.

"You are all late," he said, even though he'd arrived only seconds earlier.

A cold wind spiraled in.

The Nameless One walked through it — or perhaps the wind carried him.

His presence caused three Sirocco warriors to forget why they had drawn their weapons.

Last came the storm.

The Tempestborn didn't walk — he descended.

Lightning crawled across his armor, thunder humming inside his chest.

The Unheard stepped forward first.

"We are gathered," he whispered, and though the words were soft, they traveled across the plateau like stones skipping across water.

"The tear in the sky," he continued. "We all saw it."

"Yes," the Scorched Sovereign said. "And felt it."

"It was a message," the Nameless One added. "Something is waking."

"Something old," Zephyr muttered.

Lightning cracked across the Tempestborn's shoulder. "Something that never should have been sealed."

A silence — heavy, dark, waiting — settled over them.

Kaelen felt the whisper in his bones again.
The same phrase... broken but insistent.

"...it wakes..."

He looked to the Unheard.
The leader's expression never changed, yet Kaelen sensed something in him fracture.

The Nameless One stepped forward, eyes hollow.
"Before we discuss alliances or war, let us name the threat."

"You cannot name what devours names," the Fragmented Master said.

"You cannot silence what speaks without breath," the Scorched Sovereign added.

"You cannot outrun a wind without direction," the Tempestborn growled.

The Nameless One turned slowly toward the storm warrior.

"You've fought it before, haven't you?"

The air tensed.

Zephyr warriors scattered instinctively.

Black Wisper drew silent crescents.

Sirocco hands burned with rising heat.

The Tempestborn's voice rumbled:

"I did not fight it. I survived it."

Then —

A low rumble beneath the plateau.

The ground cracked.

A faint, eerie draft slipped between the clans' feet.

Not desert wind.

Not storm.

Not whisper.

The death-wind.

Kaelen felt his name flicker.

His breath shatter.

His bones vibrate with silent warnings.

A single warrior — a Zephyr Splinter-Step — was pulled off his feet by a current that should not exist.

He screamed once.

Not in pain —

in erasure.

The wind passed through him.

His scream vanished.

His body vanished.

His name vanished.

The first casualty of the Second Storm War.

The Tempestborn raised his blade, pointing it at the tear in the sky.

"First blood has been spilled," he roared.

"The death-wind has chosen its opening."

The Unheard whispered six words that chilled Kaelen's spine:

"The war has already begun."

3   "THE BETRAYAL AT THE CONVERGENCE"
Location: The Convergence Plateau — Nightfall

S torm clouds hung low, heavy enough to touch the plateau's jagged stone outcrops. Torches burned at strange angles, their flames bending toward the center as if dragged by unseen wind.

The five clans stood apart — tense, wounded, mistrusting — but forced together by the death-wind's recent attack.

Kaelen stood behind the Unheard again, still shaken from the death-wind's last whisper. His bones felt cold. His breath felt fragmented.

The Nameless One stepped forward, frost swirling around his feet.

"We cannot fight an enemy we cannot remember," he said. "Nor can we battle a wind that refuses to stay in form. We must unite the breaths."

The Tempestborn growled at that.

"Unite? With you?"

Lightning cracked down his arm.

Zephyr flickered in and out of reality. "Your storm nearly destroyed us in the last war. Your chaos cannot be contained."

The Scorched Sovereign crossed her arms, heat shimmering from her armor.

"Contain him? We can barely stand on the same soil without conflict. Look at us."

The Unheard lifted a hand.

Even the flames dimmed.

"Unity is necessary," he whispered. "But unity is not commanded. It is chosen."

Before anyone could respond, a new wind approached — cold, sharp, hollow.

Mistral warriors tensed.

Zephyr flickered defensively.

Tempestborn snarled.

Sirocco heat pulsed outward.

Black Wisper vanished into shadows.

Kaelen felt the wind before the others did.

Not death-wind.

Not clan-wind.

A human wind.

Footsteps.

A messenger stumbled into the firelight — a young Mistral initiate, pale and trembling.

He knelt before the Nameless One.

"I... I did what you ordered."

His voice shook. "I brought your envoy... to the Black Wisper camp."

The Nameless One froze.

"I gave no such order."

Kaelen's stomach turned.

The messenger continued, "You said to exchange the terms of alliance... and then..."

He stopped.

Then screamed.

Not from pain —

from erasure.

The air around him imploded.

Wind bent inward.

The initiate's scream crushed into silence, his body dissolving into white frost.

The ground split beneath his knees.

The Nameless One stepped back in shock — genuine shock.

Zephyr warriors erupted in chaotic flicker-blades.

Sirocco shields rose.

Black Wisper executed perfect silent formations.

Tempestborn lifted his crackling blade toward the Nameless One.

"You treacherous frost ghost," he roared, "you dare erase your own—?!"

"I DID NOT," the Nameless One snarled. "This is not my wind."

But the clans did not believe him.

The betrayal had already been accepted.

The Scorched Sovereign pointed at the Nameless One.

"You took the first shot in this war."

Zephyr flickered around him in deadly arcs.

Tempestborn charged with thunder.

Sirocco unleashed heat-waves.

Black Wisper prepared their bone-silence strike.

Only Kaelen saw what really happened.

The death-wind curled around the Nameless One's feet — thin, invisible, hungry.

Kaelen's eyes widened.

"It's not him!" he shouted.

But no one listened.

The clans attacked.

The plateau erupted in chaos.

The Betrayal at the Convergence had begun.

4 "THE HUNT FOR THE NAMELESS ONE"
Location: The Frosted Expanse — Territory of Mistral

The moon hung low over the snowfields, its light swallowed by a drifting, unnatural haze. Bitter winds howled across the frozen plains — not of the Mistral, but something older, more jagged.

Kaelen stepped onto the ice, breath steadying as the cold bit into him.

The Unheard walked beside him, drifting more than stepping, shadow stretching long across the frost. Behind them marched a mixed coalition of warriors from Black Wisper, Zephyr, and Sirocco — the uneasy result of the betrayal at the Convergence.

The Tempestborn refused to join them.

He believed the Nameless One was guilty.
Others believed the opposite.

But the Nameless One had vanished — and that itself was dangerous.

Zephyr Splinter-Steps flickered ahead, scouting through broken motion. Sirocco warriors trudged silently, their heat battling the frost. Black Wisper glided across snow like ghosts.

The Unheard spoke first.

"Kaelen," he whispered, "tell me what you feel."

Kaelen hesitated.
The whisper hadn't left him since the battle — a faint, recurring echo reverberating inside his bones.

"...find... him..."

"I hear it still," Kaelen said. "The death-wind is tracking him... or leading us. I'm not sure which."

A Zephyr scout returned, flickering into existence mid-sprint.

"We've found traces of identity erosion," he said. "Names carved into snow — erased before we could read them."

"That is his technique," a Sirocco warrior growled.

"No," the scout replied. "It isn't. The pattern is fragmented. Wrong. Too violent."

A cold dread settled over the group.

Kaelen knelt beside the markings in the snow. The symbols were melted into the ice... yet rimmed with frost at the edges.

Two opposing winds had touched this place.

The Unheard examined the pattern. "The Nameless One was here," he whispered, "but his identity is becoming unstable."

Kaelen touched the ice. A shock ran up his fingers.

He saw flashes:

The Nameless One running through a white-out.

A shadow of wind tearing after him.

Names unraveling like threads.

A voice screaming without sound.

Kaelen gasped and pulled back.

"The death-wind is hunting him."

Zephyr warriors exchanged troubled glances. "Why him?" one asked.

Kaelen swallowed hard.

"Because he tried to erase the death-wind once before."

Silence gripped the frost.

The Unheard nodded slowly. "Yes. During the First Storm War, he attempted the forbidden technique — Name Reaping — against the sixth wind. It nearly broke him."

A deep tremor echoed through the ice.

Snow rose off the ground. Wind circled inward.

A distant scream ripped across the plains — not from pain, but from identity collapse.

Kaelen drew his silent crescent.

"He's close."

$$T$$HE CHASE

The group sprinted across the Frosted Expanse. Zephyr broke into fragmented leaps. Sirocco carved tunnels of heat through the snow. Black Wisper flickered like darkness cutting through the moonlight.

Kaelen kept pace with all of them — something impossible.

The whisper inside him sharpened:

"...he is fading..."

Ahead, they saw him:

The Nameless One collapsing in the snow, frost swirling violently around him in chaotic spirals. His cloak ripped. His face pale. His eyes full of terror — a rare, raw expression for someone who existed without identity.

Wind tore strips of memory from him like paper.

He saw Kaelen approaching and choked out,
"You... why can you hear it?"

Before Kaelen could answer, the death-wind struck.

A column of hollow air twisted downward, wrapping around the Nameless One, pulling at him, unraveling his form.

Zephyr Splitters darted forward, trying to break the vortex. Sirocco heatwaves clashed with frost.
Black Wisper vibrations cut the air.

Nothing worked.

Kaelen's bones vibrated painfully — but differently than before.

He heard the death-wind speak:

"...he tried to erase me..."

Lightning cracked behind them.

The Tempestborn appeared on the ridge, Stormbreaker Fang raised high.

He roared, "STAND ASIDE!"

He unleashed a storm-lash toward the vortex.

Kaelen jumped in front of it instinctively — not blocking, but redirecting it with a motion he didn't understand.

The storm bent.

The vortex shuddered.

Everyone froze.

The Tempestborn stared at Kaelen in disbelief.

"You... silenced my storm again."

The Nameless One screamed as the vortex tightened.

Kaelen made a choice.

He stepped into the death-wind.

Warriors shouted.

The Tempestborn's eyes widened.

The Unheard reached out too late.

The vortex swallowed Kaelen.

INSIDE THE DEATH-WIND
There was no color.
No direction.
No breath.
No sound.

Only a swirling void of unmade possibility.

The Nameless One floated nearby — unraveling, pieces of his identity shredding away into the gale.

Kaelen reached for him.

The wind spoke:

"...he must be unmade..."

"...he sought to erase creation..."

"...your presence is anomaly..."

"...why do you hear us..."

Kaelen answered — not aloud but with his breath:

"Because I was born without one."

The death-wind recoiled.

The vortex destabilized.

Kaelen grabbed the Nameless One's wrist.

Energy surged through him —

identity

silence

heat

storm

fragmentation

all swirling at once, recognizing him as something impossible.

Outside, the vortex exploded.

Kaelen and the Nameless One were thrown onto the snow, unconscious.

The clans stared.

The Tempestborn whispered:

"What... are you?"

The Unheard whispered back:

"The beginning of the end."

5   "THE NAMELESS TRUTH"
Location: The Abandoned Frost Monastery
Deep within the Mistral Expanse

Snow drifted through cracked stone windows as the storm outside clawed at the ruins. The air was cold enough to blister skin, yet inside the monastery, a strange stillness gripped the hall — the calm before a truth long buried.

Kaelen lay on a stone slab, wrapped in Zephyr cloth to stabilize the fractures in his breath. He stirred, consciousness returning in fragments. The Unheard sat beside him, silent but watchful. Shadows clung to him like loyal animals.

Across the room, the Nameless One knelt — weakened, trembling, identity unraveling at the edges. His cloak had faded from royal frost-blue to a pale, dying white.

He was dying.

Not from wounds.

From absence.

The death-wind had taken pieces of him that could not be restored.

Sirocco heat-wielder Thene stood in the corner, guarding. Zephyr scouts maintained shifting vigilance. Even a Tempest warrior, grudgingly sent by the Tempestborn, stood by the entrance.

Yet all eyes were on the Nameless One.

He raised his head as Kaelen groaned awake.

"You shouldn't be alive," he whispered.

Kaelen blinked. "I could say the same to you."

The Nameless One gave a hollow laugh — the sound brittle, like cracking ice.

The Unheard leaned forward.

"Speak, Frost Sovereign," he said softly. "Tell him what you never told us."

The Nameless One's eyes — pale, unfocused — locked onto Kaelen.

"You hear it, don't you? The sixth wind. The unmaking breath."

Kaelen nodded cautiously.

"And it knows you," the Nameless One said. "That alone changes everything."

The warriors tensed.

The Unheard remained still.

Kaelen swallowed. "Why is it hunting you?"

The Nameless One exhaled, frost spilling from between his lips.

"Because long ago... I tried to kill it."

Silence — harsh and immediate — cut through the room.

Sirocco's guard stepped forward. "Impossible. The death-wind cannot be killed."

"No," the Nameless One whispered. "But I came closer than anyone in history."

He pressed his palm to the floor. Frost rippled outward, shaping into symbols — ancient, forbidden, fractured.

Zephyr's scouts flinched at the sight.

Black Wisper agents moved closer, silently attentive.

Kaelen leaned in as the Nameless One began the truth.

T HE FIRST SECRET
        THE NAMELESS CHILD

"I was not born without a name," he said. "I surrendered mine."

The frost symbols shifted, forming a blizzard-torn mountain.

"During the First Storm War, I was nothing more than a frightened initiate. My clan had already fallen to the death-wind. Every name torn away. Every identity broken."

His voice broke.

"Do you know what it's like to see your people forget their own mothers? To watch warriors lose their memories mid-battle, screaming because they don't know who they are anymore?"

He shook his head.

"I ran. I was a coward."

Kaelen's breath halted.

The Unheard closed his eyes.

T HE SECOND SECRET
        THE FORBIDDEN RITUAL

"One night, in the heart of the blizzard, I found the ancient scripture of the Mistral:

The Rite of Perfect Erasure.

The technique capable of removing identity itself — permanently."

The frost symbols twisted into a circle with a line carved through it — the symbol of Mistral.

"I believed the death-wind thrived on identities. So I attempted to perform the ritual on it."

Zephyr's warriors gasped.

The Sirocco guard whispered, "Madness."

Even the Tempest envoy took a step back.

"Yes," the Nameless One admitted. "Madness. But desperation is indistinguishable from courage in a dying world."

He clenched his fists.

"I gathered every fragment of identity left in me... and I offered it as bait."

Kaelen's pulse quickened.

"You tried to erase the death-wind," Kaelen whispered.

"I tried," the Nameless One said.

"And I failed."

He lifted his sleeve.

His forearm flickered — not illusion, not wind.

His flesh briefly vanished, replaced by a hollow outline.

He was fading — permanently.

"The ritual worked... halfway. I tore a piece of the death-wind away, but it tore pieces of me with it. Since that day, I have been less of a man and more of a question."

The frost patterns stopped.

He looked directly at Kaelen.

"And the piece of the death-wind that I stole... belongs to you."

Kaelen's heart thundered.

"What do you mean?"

The Nameless One pointed at Kaelen's chest.

"You were born shortly after the ritual — born without a cry, born with silence where breath should be."

He shuddered.

"You are the vessel of what I tore from the sixth wind. A fragment of its essence lives in you."

Every warrior drew in breath — or lost it.

Kaelen staggered, gripping the stone slab.

"No..." he whispered.

"Yes," said the Nameless One. "That is why you can hear it. Why it spares you. Why your breath fractures reality. Why your silence bends storms."

Kaelen's vision blurred.

He felt the whisper inside him stir.

"...you were always mine..."

He nearly collapsed.

The Unheard caught him.

"Kaelen," the Unheard whispered, "listen to me. Your breath is your own."

The Nameless One shook his head.

"No. His breath belongs to the sixth wind. He is the bridge between existence and unmaking."

The tempers flared.

Zephyr flickered aggressively.

Sirocco reached for weapons.

The Tempest envoy's armor crackled.

Black Wisper tightened their formation.

Kaelen stood abruptly.

"No. I won't be its vessel. I won't become its weapon."

The Nameless One gave a sorrowful smile.

"You already are."

Kaelen stepped back, shaking.

"What does the death-wind want with me?"

The Nameless One looked at him with the last clarity left inside his fading identity.

"It wants you to choose."

6 "THE FRACTURED ALLIANCE"
Location: The Convergence Plateau
Dawn After the Monastery Incident

The sky bled pale orange across the horizon as Kaelen, the Unheard, and the remaining warriors emerged from the Frosted Expanse. Wind scraped across the plateau in uneasy spirals — no longer belonging to any single clan.

Word had already spread.

By the time they reached the Convergence, five armies waited.

Black Wisper in perfect silence

Mistral in lines of frost-blue discipline

Zephyr flickering across the stone

Sirocco burning against the cold

Tempestborn warriors rumbling with storm-pressure

The Nameless One, barely held together by identity remnants, was carried behind Kaelen, guarded by three Mistral elites who looked as terrified as they did loyal.

When Kaelen stepped forward, every wind bent toward him.

Whispers.

Silence.

Heat.

Storm.

Fragmentation.

All moving toward the same center.

He felt their pull and almost lost balance.

The clans noticed.

A murmur — real sound, shocked sound — rippled across the armies.

Only the Unheard remained unmoved, floating at Kaelen's side like a shadow without purpose.

The Tempestborn spoke first.

"Give him to me."

His voice thundered across the plateau.

Zephyr warriors flickered away from his line of sight.

Mistral braced against the force.

Sirocco heat steamed on stone.

Kaelen steadied himself.

"I'm not your prisoner," he said.

"You silenced my storms twice now," the Tempestborn growled. "No warrior — no wind — should be able to do that."

Wind cracked around his armor like snapping bones.

"You are a threat."

Kaelen swallowed but didn't step back.

The Scorched Sovereign stepped forward.

"Enough," she commanded.

"Kaelen saved the Nameless One. The death-wind would have consumed Mistral entirely."

Mistral warriors bowed their heads in icy gratitude.

"But," she added, "if he carries a piece of that wind inside him... we cannot ignore the danger."

The Unheard glided between Kaelen and the armies.

"Kaelen is not the danger," he whispered.

"He is the balance the death-wind seeks."

The Tempestborn scoffed.

"A child of silence? Balance? No. He is a crack in the world."

The Fragmented Master flickered into visibility beside the Tempestborn.

"He destabilizes reality when his breath shifts," he said with a fractured voice. "I can feel the breaks when he moves."

He turned to Kaelen.

"You are either the solution... or the catalyst."

Kaelen's heartbeat thundered in his ears.

No escape.

No lies.

No silence to hide behind.

His presence itself was now enough to divide the clans.

The Nameless One struggled to stand.

His form flickered, pieces dissolving like frost melting in reverse.

"He's not a threat," the Nameless One rasped.

"He is a bridge. The only bridge."

The Tempestborn's eyes narrowed.

"Explain."

The Nameless One turned toward the armies, voice weakening.

"In the First Storm War, I tore a fragment of the sixth wind away. It survived... inside him. That makes Kaelen the only being capable of hearing the death-wind without being unmade."

The clans erupted in overlapping shouts:

"He's the death-wind's spy!"

"He's the chosen one!"

"He's the end of us!"

"He's the salvation!"

"He's not even clan-born!"

Zephyr split and reformed in agitation.

Sirocco heated the ground.

Mistral frost spread in jagged lines.

Black Wisper remained still.

Kaelen raised his hands.

"Stop!"

The winds obeyed before the clans did.

Every warrior froze.

They stared at him — unsure if he had commanded the winds or if they had chosen him.

Kaelen felt the death-wind again, whispering at the back of his mind.

"...claim... them..."

He shook the whisper off.

"I'm not your enemy," Kaelen said softly.

"I never asked for this. But the death-wind is coming. All of us will be erased if we don't—"

A deep tremor shook the plateau.

Stone cracked beneath their feet.

The Tempestborn lifted his blade.

"Enough speaking."

Lightning split the sky.

"We form alliance here and now — or we end this anomaly before he ends us."

The armies shifted into battle stances.

Kaelen's breath stuttered —

fractured —

shattered —

And a wave of displaced wind burst from him, sending dust spiraling into a perfect hollow sphere around his body.

His eyes glowed with reflected winds — five winds at war inside him.

The Unheard placed a hand on his shoulder.

"Choose your words carefully," he whispered.

Kaelen stepped forward.

THE DECLARATION THAT FRACTURES THE CLANS
Kaelen addressed the armies:

"I will not submit.

I will not be claimed.

I will not be hunted."

The wind pulsed with every word.

"But I will fight the death-wind. And I will help any clan that chooses survival over pride."

He looked at each leader:

"To stand with me risks everything."

He turned toward the storm.

"To stand against me risks more."

The armies wavered, waiting for the first voice of support.

Sirocco moved first.

The Scorched Sovereign bowed her head.

"We choose survival. And we choose the one who survived the death-wind itself."

Half her army knelt.

The other half stepped back.

A fracture.

Zephyr flickered next.

The Fragmented Master circled Kaelen once, studying the broken motion of his breath.

"I choose curiosity," he said. "I choose the impossible."

A third of Zephyr joined Kaelen.

Another fracture.

Black Wisper stepped behind Kaelen.

"We were always with him," the Unheard said.

Their entire army formed a silent wall behind him.

Mistral split.

Half believed the Nameless One's truth.

The other half believed Kaelen was a living weapon that must be destroyed.

Frost cracked violently in the divide.

Tempest refused.

The Tempestborn pointed Stormbreaker Fang at Kaelen.

"I choose war."

Lightning speared the sky.

Thunder erupted.

Tempest warriors rallied behind him in full formation.

The plateau trembled under the weight of the choice.

Five clans.

One child of silence.

Four fractured alliances.

One inevitable war.

Kaelen took a shaky breath.

The wind answered with thunder, frost, silence, heat, and fractured motion all spiraling toward him.

The Unheard whispered:

"This is the moment the prophecy warned us of."

7 "THE BREAKING OF STORM AND FROST"
Location: The Icebound Rift
Border between Mistral and Tempest Territories

The Icebound Rift was a scar across the world — a frozen canyon carved centuries ago by the Tempestborn during the First Storm War. Wind currents here clashed violently, frost and lightning grinding against each other like ancient enemies.

It was here the first true battle of the new war ignited.

I. The Tempest March

Stormborn warriors advanced in formation, their armor humming with unstable lightning. The Tempestborn himself walked ahead of them, Stormbreaker Fang dragging across the ice, leaving a scorched groove in the frost.

Each step he took shattered the frozen ground.

Each breath he exhaled twisted the clouds above.

"We end this tonight," he said.

"No more fragments. No more whispers. No more lies."

Tempest warriors roared in thunderous approval.

The sky responded with lightning.

II. The Alliance Arrives

Kaelen stood at the opposite end of the rift, flanked by:

The Unheard and the full Black Wisper cohort

The Scorched Sovereign with half her Sirocco warriors

The Fragmented Master and a flickering Zephyr detachment

And behind them, the fractured half of Mistral loyal to the Nameless One

Snow whipped around them.

Frost cracked under their feet.

Zephyr flickers danced like broken light.

Kaelen's heart pounded.

He had never led an army — he had barely led himself.

But the winds moved toward him.

They recognized him.

Feared him.

Followed him.

The Unheard leaned close.

"Do not command the winds," he whispered. "Invite them."

Kaelen nodded.

Across the battlefield, the Tempestborn raised his storm-cracked blade.

"Child of silence," he thundered, "face me."

A roar of approval echoed from the stormborn ranks.

Sirocco warriors raised shields of heat.

Mistral conjured white-out blizzards.

Black Wisper dissolved into shadow.

Zephyr blurred between realities.

The rift cracked louder.

The battle was a breath away.

III. The First Strike — Frost vs. Storm

The Nameless One staggered forward, frost leaking from his fingers.

Despite his fading form, he still wielded devastating power.

"Mistral—!" he shouted.

His remaining warriors responded instantly.

They unleashed Erasure Gale, a freezing crosswind meant to slice into Tempest ranks and disrupt storm pressure.

The Tempestborn countered.

"Stormlash!"

Lightning erupted, spiraling across the battlefield like a serpent of raw force.

Frost collided with storm.

The impact shattered the rift floor, sending shards of ice the size of houses spiraling into the air.

Kaelen shielded his face as the shockwave tore past him.

Two winds collided —

neither winning, both breaking.

This was the Breaking of Storm and Frost.

IV. The Tempestborn Advances

Tempest warriors surged forward, storm-pressure amplifying their every step.

A wall of lightning formed behind them.

Thunder struck the ice with such force the fissures widened into a cavernous abyss.

Zephyr reacted first.

"Scatter!"

Splinter-Steps flickered across the battlefield in fragmented arcs, slashing at Tempest ranks.

But lightning followed them, tracking their motions with storm sense.

Many Zephyr warriors were dragged out of their broken steps by sudden lightning bursts, collapsing mid-flicker.

The Fragmented Master cursed.

"We cannot outpace a storm that remembers us!"

V. The Black Wisper Counter

The Unheard lifted his hand.

"Silence the storm."

His warriors spread out, forming a shifting circle around the Tempestborn's forces.

They exhaled — not sound, but silence.

A dome of deadened air expanded outward.

Lightning dimmed.

Thunder faltered.

Even the Tempestborn's breathing seemed muffled.

But the stormborn pushed through.

Lightning cracked violently, shattering the silence dome into a thousand invisible shards.

The Unheard staggered.

Kaelen caught him.

"He's too strong," Kaelen said.

"No," whispered the Unheard. "The storm is too angry."

VI. Sirocco's Turn — Heat Against the Blizzard

The Scorched Sovereign stepped forward, flames erupting from her arms.

"Sirocco!" she bellowed.
"Break the frost!"

Heatwaves blasted across the field, melting snow, weakening Mistral's white-out veil.
Steam turned the battlefield into a boiling fog.

But the Tempestborn welcomed the heat —
lightning feeds on rising air.

He raised his blade.

"Tempest Breach!"

Lightning struck the ground in a jagged circle, vaporizing the steam and blowing Sirocco warriors backward.

The Scorched Sovereign slid across the ice, armor cracking.

Kaelen rushed to her.

She grabbed his wrist.

"Do not hold back," she whispered.

VII. The Turning Point — Kaelen's Breath Breaks

The Tempestborn pointed his blade directly at Kaelen.

"You carry the sixth wind," he growled. "I will not allow that wind to choose you."

He unleashed a stormburst aimed solely at Kaelen.

Kaelen's instincts took over.

He inhaled —
felt silence
felt frost

felt heat
felt fragmentation
felt storm
and exhaled a single, fractured breath.
The world broke.
Wind exploded in a sphere around him.
Tempest lightning bent away.
Mistral frost deflected.
Zephyr flickers stabilized.
Sirocco heat dissolved into controlled currents.
Black Wisper silence thickened into armor.
Kaelen stood in the center of a five-wind vortex —
his eyes glowing,
his breath shimmering with impossible contradiction.
A hybrid wind.
Something the world had never seen.
The battlefield froze.
The Tempestborn stared in disbelief.
"What... are you becoming?"
Kaelen's voice echoed with layered winds.
"I don't know."
The death-wind whispered through the battlefield:
"...he is the convergence..."

VIII. The Clash of Leaders

The Tempestborn charged.
Stormbreaker Fang crackled with fury.
Kaelen braced, instinctively pulling the winds into his body.
Their weapons collided —
LIGHTNING.
SILENCE.
HEAT.
FROST.

FRAGMENTS.
VOID.
The explosion shook the entire rift.
Ice cliffs shattered.
Storm clouds ripped open.
The ground split into new canyons.
Kaelen flew backward, skidding across the ice.
He coughed, shaking.
The Tempestborn staggered too, armor cracked, lightning sputtering.
"You..." he growled.
"...are not natural."
Kaelen stood.
"No. I'm necessary."
The Tempestborn roared and prepared a killing blow—
But a sudden scream cut through the battlefield:
"KAELEN!"
The Nameless One collapsed, his body unraveling completely.
His form dissolved into frost particles that blew away across the snow.
His final whisper echoed:
"...it's coming..."
The death-wind spiraled into existence above the battlefield
—
vast
shifting
hollow
hungry.
The clans froze as its voice descended:
"...choose your side... before I erase your world..."

8 "THE WIND THAT DEVOURS ARMIES"
Location: The Icebound Rift
Immediately Following the Death-Wind's Descent

The sky split open.
Not with lightning.
Not with storm.
Not with breath or frost or heat.

But with absence.

A hollow wind spiraled above the battlefield, darker than shadow yet brighter than void, a shimmering distortion that bent the world around it. Zephyr flickers died mid-step. Sirocco heat froze. Black Wisper silence shattered. Mistral snow fell upward. Even Tempest lightning recoiled.

The death-wind had arrived.

Wind did not blow.

Wind unwound.

Kaelen staggered to one knee. His lungs tightened. His breath trembled, not from fear—but resonance.

The death-wind whispered:

"...war is irrelevant...

...you are all fractures waiting to be erased..."

A Tempest warrior screamed as his shadow detached from his feet and dissolved. His body followed—erased from existence, leaving only a crack in the ice where he once stood.

Panic tore through the ranks.

Zephyr splintered in random directions.

Sirocco heatwaves sputtered out.

Mistral frost lost cohesion.

Tempestborn warriors lost their storm sense entirely.

The battlefield became pure chaos.

The Unheard shouted—actual sound, rare and terrifying:

"FORMATION! NOW!"

Black Wisper warriors moved instantly, forming a circle around Kaelen. Silence thickened, but even their greatest technique could not fully block the death-wind.

Kaelen felt it tug at him—gently, insistently.

"...return what is mine..."

He clutched his chest, breath fracturing.

The Tempestborn roared from across the field.

"YOU WILL NOT TAKE HIM!"

Stormbreaker Fang surged with lightning as he charged the vortex.

"Stormbirth!"

He unleashed a tempest explosion powerful enough to fracture mountains...

...but the death-wind ate it.

Simply consumed the storm, absorbing it as if swallowing a candle flame.

The Tempestborn skidded backward in disbelief.

"No..." he whispered. "No wind devours storm."

The death-wind's voice deepened:

"...storm is merely breath...

...I am the void between breaths..."

A second gust ripped outward—silent yet catastrophic.

Thirty warriors vanished instantly.

Their armor clattered onto the ice without bodies inside.

Zephyr warriors flickered to escape but flickered into nothing.

Mistral blades turned to frost-dust.

Sirocco shields cracked and collapsed.

Even the Unheard trembled.

"Kaelen," he whispered. "If you do not intervene, all will be lost."

Kaelen shook violently.

"I don't know how."

"You do," the Unheard said. "The wind chose you."

THE DEATH-WIND STRIKES

The death-wind descended lower, sucking entire chunks of battlefield into its center.

A vortex formed at the heart of the rift—an absence storm.

Warriors screamed.

Stones dissolved.

Frozen cliffs peeled away like sheets of old parchment.

The Tempestborn threw himself into the vortex, lightning exploding from his armor as he tried to hold it back.

"I will NOT lose again!" he roared.

But even he was forced to his knees.

The Fragmented Master flickered beside Kaelen, erratic and panicked.

"This is not wind…"

He flickered to the left.

"…this is not storm…"

He flickered behind Kaelen.

"…this is unwind…"

He disappeared mid-sentence—

then reappeared, gasping, as if pulled through different layers of existence.

"Kaelen—your breath interacts with it. You must shape it. Before it shapes us."

Kaelen inhaled sharply.

The death-wind reacted immediately.

The vortex shifted toward him.

Every clan warrior screamed, "NO!"

KAELEN ENTERS THE UNWIND

Kaelen stepped forward alone.

Not to run.

Not to hide.

To listen.

He let his breath synchronize with the sixth wind—silence, storm, heat, frost, fragmentation—every wind he'd felt bending into chaotic harmony.

The death-wind whispered:

"...you are my missing breath..."

Kaelen's eyes darkened.

The vortex swirled around him like a crown of absence.

The Tempestborn shouted across the battlefield:

"KAELEN! DO NOT LET IT CLAIM YOU!"

But Kaelen no longer heard the armies.

He heard the truth.

"...you are the fragment I lost...

...you are the bridge between breath and unbreath..."

Kaelen reached out his hand.

The death-wind's core twisted, spiraled, and folded inward—

—and Kaelen stepped into it.

The world vanished.

INSIDE THE DEATH-WIND

There was no sky.

No earth.

No direction.

Only a swirling void of undone things:

erased names

forgotten faces

broken breaths

unspoken histories

Kaelen floated at the center of the unmaking.

A figure shaped itself from the void—

not man, not wind, not god.

A silhouette made of absence.

It spoke with every voice ever erased:

"You will decide which world remains.

Not the clans.

Not the storm.

Not the first winds.

Only you."

Kaelen trembled.

"Why me?"

"Because you were born from my missing piece.

Because they all fear you.

Because you are the first being meant to shape wind and un-winding."

Kaelen tried to step back—there was no ground.

"No... I'm not your vessel. I'm not your weapon."

"Correct."

Kaelen froze.

The death-wind leaned close—though it had no face.

"You are my equal."

The vortex around him pulsed violently, as if the world outside were being shredded.

"Speak, child of silence.

Will I devour this world...

or will you fight me for it?"

Kaelen's breath fractured—silence bending around him.

He whispered:

"I choose neither."

The death-wind hissed.

Kaelen continued:

"I will not let you erase the world...

and I will not let the clans destroy each other.

I will break the fate you wrote."

For the first time, the death-wind hesitated.

He spoke the words it had never encountered:

"I refuse your destiny."

The void shuddered.

Reality trembled.

The death-wind roared.

OUTSIDE — THE ARMIES WATCH

The vortex exploded outward—

not with destruction,

but with silence.

A dome of stillness expanded from the rift.

The armies staggered.

The Tempestborn shielded his eyes.

The Unheard whispered:

"He's rewriting the wind."

Sirocco heat rose.

Mistral frost crackled.

Zephyr flickers steadied.

Tempeststorms bent inward.

The dome collapsed—

—and Kaelen fell from the sky, unconscious but alive.

The battlefield was eerily untouched.

Warriors gasped.

The death-wind was gone.

Not defeated.

Not destroyed.

Gone.

For now.

Kaelen lay in the snow, breathing faintly.

The Tempestborn stared at him with a mixture of fear and awe.

"He did what even the storm could not."

The Unheard knelt beside Kaelen, brushing frost from his face.

"He broke the wind that devours armies," he whispered.

"Now the question becomes...

What will the wind break next?"

9   "THE SHATTERED PEACE"
Location: The Broken Sanctuary
Neutral Ground Outside the Rift
Three Days After the Battle

K aelen awoke to silence.

Not the familiar silence of the Black Wisper.
Not the deadly silence of the death-wind.

A fragile silence — like the world was holding its breath.

He lay in a small healing chamber carved from ancient stone, light filtering down through slits in the ceiling. Sirocco heat-stones warmed the air. Frost charms hung from Mistral strings to keep his breath stable. Zephyr fragments whispered faintly in the corners. A single Black Wisper candle flickered without flame.

Five winds.
One room.

He sat up slowly, body aching in places that didn't exist before the battle.

"You're awake," came a voice.

The Unheard drifted into view, his presence soft as always. But his eyes... held weight Kaelen had never seen.

"What happened?" Kaelen asked.

"You stopped a war," the Unheard whispered. "And started another."

Kaelen swallowed hard.

"Is the death-wind gone?"

The Unheard hesitated.

"It retreated. It was not defeated."

Kaelen closed his eyes. "I failed."

"No," the Unheard said. "You changed it. You altered the breath of the unbreath. That has never been done."

Kaelen wasn't sure whether to feel pride or terror.

I. The Leaders Arrive

Footsteps echoed outside.

Not hurried.

Not hostile.

Measured.

The door slid open.

One by one, they entered:

The Scorched Sovereign, armor cracked but eyes steady.

The Fragmented Master, flickering in controlled intervals.

The Nameless One's Second, a tall Mistral warrior wrapped in frost silk.

A Tempest envoy, not the Tempestborn himself — a sign of insult and caution.

They formed a semicircle around Kaelen's resting place.

The Scorched Sovereign spoke first.

"You changed the outcome of that battle," she said. "Without you, none of us would be standing here."

Kaelen shook his head. "I didn't do it alone."

"No," the Tempest envoy said coldly. "You did something worse."

Kaelen stiffened. "Worse?"

"You unbalanced the Six Winds," he replied. "You blended them. That is... unnatural."

Zephyr flickered once, then clarified:

"Impossible."

The Mistral representative stepped forward.

"And dangerous."

Kaelen felt the tension rising like a held breath.

"What are you saying?"

The Tempest envoy pointed a crackling gauntlet at him.

"You are the reason the death-wind targeted the armies. You drew it. You provoked it. You—"

The Unheard cut him off.

"He saved all of you."

"And nearly destroyed the world doing it!" the envoy snapped.

Zephyr's leader flickered uncertainly.

Sirocco's Sovereign looked conflicted.

Mistral's warrior raised a hand.

"There is more," he said. "The Nameless One... left a message before he unraveled."

Kaelen's heart stilled.

"What message?"

The warrior produced a fragment of frost — glowing faintly, trembling.

"He said the death-wind has begun to... notice something."

"Notice what?" Kaelen asked.

The frost fragment pulsed once.

Then twice.

Then the warrior spoke the final words:

"It notices you."

II. The Council Fractures

The Unheard remained calm.

"We cannot ignore Kaelen's role. He is part of the prophecy. The Listener. The bridge. The—"

The Tempest envoy slammed a fist into the stone.

"He is a threat. A living crack in the world!"

Zephyr nodded slightly.

Mistral's eyes narrowed.

Sirocco clenched a fist.

Kaelen stepped forward.

"I'm not your enemy."

The room's winds shifted involuntarily at his voice — silence thickening, frost sharpening, heat rising, fragments flickering, storm-pressure bending.

All five winds responded.

The leaders recoiled.

"You see?" the Tempest envoy hissed. "He doesn't control the winds — the winds control him."

"That's not true," Kaelen argued.

But even he wasn't sure.

The Sirocco Sovereign spoke gently.

"Kaelen... we need to know what you are becoming."

Kaelen felt heat in his chest. "I don't know."

The Zephyr leader flickered into five forms.

"That is the problem."

The Unheard stepped between Kaelen and the others.

"We need unity now more than ever."

"No," the Tempest envoy snapped. "What we need... is containment."

Kaelen tensed. "Containment?"

"Yes," the envoy said. "Until we understand your nature, you cannot lead, cannot fight, cannot wander free. You are either a weapon... or a disaster."

Sirocco looked away.

Mistral remained silent.

Zephyr's flicker slowed.

The fractured alliance had begun to crumble.

III. Kaelen Makes a Choice

Kaelen stepped backward, breath shaking.

"I risked everything to save you."

"And you may doom us all," the envoy said.

Kaelen's hands curled into fists.

"Say you want me dead," he whispered.

The envoy didn't hesitate.

"Some of us do."

Sirocco inhaled sharply.

Zephyr flickered nervously.

Mistral spoke softly:

"But not all."

The Unheard turned to Kaelen.

"You must decide now. Do you stay with the alliance... or go your own way?"

Kaelen looked at the leaders.

At the fear.

At the fractured trust.

At the storm gathering in the distance.

"I won't let you cage me," he said quietly.

The envoy snarled. "Then you choose rebellion!"

Kaelen shook his head.

"I choose the truth."

He turned toward the exit.

"The death-wind is coming again. And it won't care about alliances or battles. It wants only one thing—balance."

He paused.

"And I'm the only one who can hear what kind of balance it seeks."

Sirocco stepped forward.

"Where will you go?"

Kaelen glanced at the horizon.

"To the place where the winds were born," he said. "To find the truth the clans refused to face."

The Unheard nodded.

"I will go with you."

Zephyr hesitated, then flickered in agreement.

Mistral's warrior bowed slightly.

Tempest's envoy scoffed. "Run, then. The Tempestborn will hunt you."

Kaelen stepped into the wind.

"Let him try."

He vanished in a broken-motion burst—

not Zephyr

not Wisper

not Sirocco

not Tempest

not Mistral

—but all of them.

For a long moment, no one spoke.

The Scorched Sovereign finally sighed.

"The peace is shattered," she said.

Mistral nodded. "And the war has begun."

The Tempest envoy snarled:

"We hunt the anomaly."

The Unheard whispered:

"No.

You hunt the prophecy."

1 0

"HUNTED BY THE TEMPESTBORN"

Location: The Windless Barrens

Southern Expanse

K aelen ran.
Not with Zephyr's broken stride.
Not with Wisper's silent glide.
Not with Sirocco's steady heat.
Not with Mistral's drifting pace.
Not with Tempest's thunderbound charge.
He ran with something new —
a step that bent the wind into a quiet fracture behind him.
Footprints formed without sound.
Shadows flickered without light.
Breath condensed without cold.
The Unheard glided behind him, perfectly noiseless.
Two Zephyr Splinter-Steps flickered ahead as scouts.
Sirocco envoy Thene trailed them, heat-waves obscuring their retreat.
But the storm followed.
A bruise-colored cloud rolled across the sky, lightning crawling inside it like veins of anger. The air vibrated with the thunderous cadence of a hunter's will.
The Tempestborn had found them.
Thene cursed under her breath.
"He shouldn't be able to track us this fast."
"He isn't tracking us," Kaelen said.
"He's tracking me."

The Unheard drifted closer.

"Kaelen, your breath signature has changed. It calls to every wind — and storms are the most aggressive responders."

A lightning spear slammed into the sand beside them — exploding it into molten glass.

Zephyr scouts flickered away from the blast, shouting.

"He's descending!"

A massive silhouette dropped from the clouds.

Stormbreaker Fang split the air with a crack that rattled Kaelen's bones.

The Tempestborn landed hard, thunder rolling across the barrens.

Lightning crawled across his armor like living serpents.

"Kaelen!" he roared. "You stand between the world and oblivion — and I will NOT let the sixth wind claim you!"

Kaelen stepped forward, chest heaving.

"I'm not claimed."

"You are changing," the Tempestborn snapped. "And the clans cannot risk what you'll become."

He lowered Stormbreaker Fang.

"This is mercy, not execution."

Lightning built behind him — a storm ready to erupt.

He charged.

Kaelen inhaled—

and the death-wind whispered in his lungs:

"...let me help..."

Kaelen jerked back in fear.

"No."

He exhaled instead —

a fractured breath.

Silence cracked.

Storm buckled.

Wind folded.

The Tempestborn slammed into an invisible distortion and skidded across the sand.

Thunder stuttered in the clouds.

He rose, shocked.

"What... was that?"

Kaelen stared at his hands.

"I think," he whispered, "that was me refusing you."

The Tempestborn let out a howl of fury.

Lightning erupted around him.

He charged again—

and this time, Kaelen braced.

Their winds collided.

Silence vs. Thunder.

Frost vs. Heat.

Fragment vs. Force.

Unbirth vs. Stormbirth.

The explosion shook the world.

Kaelen flew back, crashing into a dune.

He coughed blood.

The Tempestborn staggered too, armor cracking from the impact.

"Your breath..." he growled, "...it is correcting mine."

Kaelen rose shakily.

"I don't want to fight you."

"You have no choice!" the Tempestborn roared.

"I always have a choice," Kaelen said. "That's what the death-wind hates."

Lightning surged again—

but Zephyr Splinter-Steps intervened, flickering between Kaelen and the Tempestborn.

Sirocco heatwaves blasted the sand, obscuring vision.

The Unheard summoned a dome of silence.

"Retreat!" he shouted — the rare sound slicing the air.

Kaelen was dragged into a flicker-step.
The world shattered and reformed around them.
They vanished.
The Tempestborn slammed the ground in fury—
thunder ripping the desert in half.

1

"THE SILENT ECHO"
Location: The Edge of the World
The Abyssal Cliffs

Night fell without stars.

Kaelen and the small band of allies staggered to the cliffs — an ancient region where the world's winds did not behave normally.

Below them yawned a chasm so deep the bottom was hidden in pale mist.

Above them hung a sky split by faint fractures — the scars left from Kaelen's confrontation with the death-wind.

Thene dropped to one knee, exhausted.

Zephyr scouts flickered uncontrollably, their steps unstable.

The Unheard hovered silently behind Kaelen, as if sensing the next revelation before it arrived.

Kaelen stared at the abyss.

"Where are we?" he asked.

The Unheard answered softly:

"The place where the winds were born.
And the place where they end."

Kaelen stepped closer.

The air was wrong here.
Too still.
Too ancient.
As if the world itself had stopped breathing.

The Unheard continued:

"If you seek truth, Kaelen, this is where you must begin."

Kaelen swallowed.

"What truth?"

The Unheard looked at him — really looked — for the first time in the entire journey.

"The truth of your birth."

A cold wind rolled across the cliff — not death-wind, not clan-wind.

Something older.

Something watching.

Kaelen's breath hitched.

"Tell me."

The Unheard nodded slowly.

"Your mother came here once.

Before you were born."

Kaelen froze.

"She walked into the abyss," the Unheard said, "and returned carrying a breath that did not belong to this world."

Kaelen's eyes widened.

"No..."

"Yes," the Unheard whispered.

"You were not merely born without a cry...

You were born carrying the fragment the Nameless One tore away."

Kaelen trembled.

"Then what am I?"

The Unheard drifted forward, placing a hand on Kaelen's shoulder.

"Not wind. Not un-wind. Not clan. Not void."

He pointed toward the abyss.

"You are what lies between them."

The cliffs rumbled.

Cracks split across the stone.

Wind spiraled upward in unnatural currents.

The abyss began to glow.

Kaelen staggered back.

"What is happening?"

The Unheard whispered:

"The death-wind has awakened because you have."

The earth shook.

Thunder roared from somewhere deep inside the chasm.

A voice rose — not wind, not storm, not silence, but all of them twisted together:

"...LISTENER..."

Kaelen fell to his knees as the abyss screamed his title:

"...THE WORLD AWAITS YOUR CHOICE..."

The cliff crumbled beneath them.

Kaelen dangled over the void, wind whipping past him like claws.

He looked up at the Unheard — and saw fear in his eyes for the first time.

"Kaelen!" the Unheard shouted. "Listen—"

The ground shattered.

Kaelen fell into the abyss.

The world went silent.

Part II

1 "DESCENT INTO THE FIRST BREATH"
Location: The Abyssal Deep
Below the Edge of the World

K aelen fell.
Not downward.
Not upward.
Not through wind or gravity.
He fell through breath.
The world above dissolved into streaks of fractured light.
Time stretched and snapped.
Shadows moved independently of his body.
His heartbeat echoed like distant thunder inside a hollow world.
He tried to scream—
—but no sound formed.
Not because he was silenced.
Because sound did not exist here.
The abyss swallowed everything except one thing:
identity.
And even that began to unravel.
Kaelen clutched his chest.
His breath flickered — not steady, not stable, but shifting through five winds at once.
Silence. Frost. Heat. Fragment. Storm.
His vision warped.
Then—
He stopped falling.
Not on ground.
Not in water.
Not in air.

He hovered in a void that shimmered like liquid starlight.
And then he heard it.
Breathing.
Ancient breathing.
Not from one being.
From many.

I. The Primordial Winds Awaken

Shapes formed out of the shimmering void.
Not humanoid.
Not monstrous.
Not of any clan.

These were the winds before clans existed.

The Primordial Winds.

Their forms were fluid, drifting like tapestries of color and motion.

The Quiet One: A being of total stillness. A silhouette carved from silence itself. Its very presence erased sound.

The Remembering Current: A spiraling form made of overlapping memories and whispers. Its glow carried voices from times long gone.

The Broken Zephyr: A creature of fragments, its limbs shifting through different positions faster than sight. It existed in several places at once.

The Forsaken Gale: A wind-being made of heat ripples and desert mirages.
Its body warred between burning and fading.

The First Tempest: A towering mass of stormfire and crackling cloud. Lightning coiled around its core like serpents.

And then—

The Unbreath

Not a form.
A void where a form should be.

The absence of wind.

The hunger between existence and nonexistence.

Kaelen staggered backward, breath shaking.

"What... are you?"

The Quiet One moved without motion, its form bending into a shape resembling a bowed head.

"...we... are the first..."

The voices of the Primordial Winds blended, layered, ancient.

"...before clans... before seals... before war... we shaped the world..."

Kaelen's chest tightened.

"You created the winds?"

"...we are the winds..."

said the Remembering Current.

"...and you... Kaelen... are of us..."

said the Forsaken Gale.

Kaelen froze.

"No," he whispered. "I'm human."

The First Tempest crackled.

"...half... perhaps..."

The Broken Zephyr flickered behind him.

"...but your breath is not..."

Kaelen's pulse hammered.

He felt small.

Childlike.

Exposed.

"Why am I here? Why did I fall into this place?"

The Unbreath pulsed — a ripple of absence that bent the void.

For the first time, Kaelen heard its voice clearly:

"...to finish what was begun..."

II. The Truth of the First Breath

The Remembering Current spiraled around Kaelen, whispering through centuries past.

Images flooded his mind:

a world without clans

winds roaming freely

storms that carried no death

breaths that shaped mountains

silence that healed

motion without fragmentation

heat that gave life

unbreath that balanced creation

Then—

A fracture.

A single flaw in reality.

The clans were born from this flaw.

But so was something else.

The Unbreath.

The death-wind.

Kaelen fell to his knees.

"You mean... the clans weren't supposed to exist?"

The First Tempest flared angrily.

"...the clans took fragments of us..."

The Quiet One added:

"...they used our breaths... severed our unity..."

The Broken Zephyr crackled:

"...creation fractured... war followed..."

Kaelen's breath stuttered.

"So the clans caused the First Storm War."

"...yes..."

"And the death-wind emerged to restore balance."

The Unbreath pulsed once.

"...balance... or erasure... depending on resistance..."

Kaelen clenched his fists.

"What do you want from me?"

The Primordial Winds circled him slowly, their combined presence overwhelming but somehow familiar.

"...you carry our missing breath..."

said the Quiet One.

"...the piece the Nameless One stole..."

said the Remembering Current.

"...the fragment the sixth wind lost..."

said the Broken Zephyr.

"...the only piece with choice..."

said the Forsaken Gale.

Kaelen felt his chest burn.

"Choice..." he whispered. "I told the death-wind I wouldn't follow its destiny."

The First Tempest's lightning dimmed.

"...and in doing so... you awakened your own..."

Kaelen looked up.

"What destiny?"

The Primordial Winds answered as one:

"...to become what we once were...

...the Seventh Wind..."

The void trembled at their words.

Kaelen shook his head.

"No. I can't. I'm not—"

The Unbreath surged forward, its presence swallowing light.

"...you are what remains of the wind we lost...

...you are the breath that bridges all winds...

...you are the Listener...

...the Decider...

...the one who may silence or restore the world..."

Kaelen's hands shook uncontrollably.

"I'm just a boy."

The Quiet One approached, placing a shape-like hand upon his shoulder.

"...all winds begin as breath...

...even the first..."

Kaelen felt tears in his eyes.

"Why me?"

The Primordial Winds answered in a whisper that shook the void:

"...because the world has forgotten how to breathe...

...and only you can teach it again..."

III. Kaelen's True Potential Awakens

The Primordial Winds began to dissolve their forms, swirling together like a galaxy of motion, silence, storm, heat, frost, and void.

They spiraled toward Kaelen.

His breath caught—

painful, burning—

Then—

His lungs expanded with impossible force.

Wind surged through him.

Silence wrapped around him.

Heat fused with frost.

Fragmentation stabilized.

Storm coiled inside him.

Unbreath resonated with his pulse.

Kaelen screamed—

But no sound came out.

Instead, the void cracked open with a new wind:

a Seventh Breath.

A wind that had never existed before.

A wind that did not steal, destroy, or dominate—

But balanced.

A harmonizing force.

The Primordial Winds bowed.

The Unbreath whispered:

"...you are not my enemy...

...you are my completion..."

Kaelen rose slowly, glowing with a wind no being had ever seen.

"I am not your vessel," he whispered.

"Nor your weapon."

He inhaled—

—and the void trembled.

"I am the Seventh Wind."

Light consumed the abyss.

2 "RISE OF THE SEVENTH WIND"
Location: The Abyssal Cliffs
Moments After the Transformation

Light tore upward from the abyss.
Not lightning.
Not storm.
Not frost, heat, or silence.
Something else.
A wind that shimmered with contradictory hues — calm yet violent, quiet yet roaring, whole yet fractured. The ground trembled as the abyss exhaled a breath the world had never felt.
Zephyr scouts stumbled back in terror.
Sirocco warriors raised shields of heat.
Mistral exiles kneeled in instinctive reverence.
Black Wisper agents vanished into shadow.
The Tempestborn halted mid-stride, his storm suddenly uncertain.
The abyss cracked open—
And Kaelen rose from the chasm.
Not climbing.
Not levitating.
Rising on wind that obeyed only him.
His cloak fluttered in currents that spiraled impossibly.
His eyes flickered with shifting winds.
His breath glowed faintly with unbreath resonance.
His presence bent the air—
not by force, but by harmony.
The Unheard whispered, breath trembling:
"Kaelen... what have you become?"

Kaelen touched the cliff's surface.

Wind rippled through the stone, stabilizing the crumbling edge.

"I became what the world needed," he said softly.

Sirocco's Sovereign stepped back.

Mistral's warrior froze.

Even Zephyr's flicker stopped entirely.

The Tempestborn, who had arrived moments before the eruption, stared at him with a mixture of awe and dread.

"This... is not possible," he said.

"No wind can contain all others."

Kaelen exhaled.

Wind bent around him in perfect spirals.

"I don't contain them," Kaelen said, voice layered with multiple breaths.

"I balance them."

I. The Primordial Winds' Warning

The world shimmered.

For a moment, all six Primordial Winds appeared behind Kaelen — barely visible, shapes made of memory and ancient breath.

The Quiet One:

"...beware the storm..."

The Remembering Current:

"...he remembers the old war... and fears the new wind..."

The Broken Zephyr:

"...the Tempestborn fractures under destiny..."

The Forsaken Gale:

"...his heat turns to ruin..."

The First Tempest thundered a warning:

"...the storm fears replacement..."

And the Unbreath whispered its final message:

"...the Tempestborn will break the world...

...unless you break his storm..."

Kaelen trembled slightly.

"They fear him?" he asked.

The Primordial Winds answered as one:

"...no...

...they fear what he will do

when he realizes

he cannot control you..."

The Tempestborn's face twisted.

"You speak to ghosts and forgotten winds," he growled. "The clans are the world. Not them. Not you. Us."

Kaelen shook his head.

"No. The clans are fragments. They were never meant to carry whole breaths."

The Tempestborn's armor crackled violently.

"You insult our ancestors."

"No," Kaelen said. "I correct them."

The Tempestborn roared in fury—and fear.

II. The Clans' Reaction to the Return of Kaelen

The leaders and warriors whispered, uncertain.

Sirocco's Reaction

Thene stepped forward hesitantly.

"Kaelen... the air around you... it feels like dawn and dusk at once."

Her sovereign bowed her head.

"You carry heat without burning. Wind without cutting. Balance without weakness. No Sirocco warrior has seen such a breath."

Zephyr's Reaction

Fragmented Master flickered around Kaelen, studying him.

"You stabilize fractures. My broken path is clear near you. You unbreak my steps."

He flickered again, this time without distortion.

"This is... terrifying."

Mistral's Reaction

The Mistral representative knelt.

"You carry the wind our Nameless One feared and longed for. You are neither identity nor erasure—you are clarity."

Kaelen shivered.

"I don't know what I am."

Black Wisper's Reaction

The Unheard bowed, deeply.

"You are the prophecy fulfilled. The wind that listens. The breath that decides."

Kaelen felt a heavy weight with those words.

Tempest's Reaction

The Tempestborn lifted his blade in open challenge.

"You are a threat to the world's order."

Kaelen stepped forward calmly.

"No. You are a threat to its future."

Lightning exploded across the cliffside.

III. The New Prophecy of the Seventh Breath

A wind swept across the cliff —

not Kaelen's,

not the Primordial Winds',

not the clans'.

A wind older than prophecy itself.

It carved symbols into the stone:

**"When six are broken

a seventh rises.

Neither storm nor silence,

neither flame nor frost,

neither fractured nor erased.

The Seventh Breath shall stand

between creation and uncreation.

If he silences the storm,

the world survives.

If he joins the unbreath,

the world renews.

If he falls to fear,

all winds end."**

The stone cracked.

The prophecy vanished.

Kaelen stared at the now-broken surface.

"That's... about me?"

The Unheard nodded solemnly.

"Yes. And the final line carries the weight of all existence."

The Tempestborn raised his blade.

"Then we cannot allow the Seventh Wind to grow unchecked."

Kaelen's eyes hardened.

"I didn't ask for this."

The Tempestborn answered:

"Destiny doesn't require your permission."

IV. The Seventh Wind Emerges

Kaelen took a slow breath.

Wind spiraled behind him —

seven currents aligning,

seven breaths harmonizing,

seven winds bowing to his presence.

The Tempestborn took a step back for the first time.

Kaelen said:

"I will not be your enemy.

But I will not be your prisoner.

And I will not let you decide the fate of this world."

The Seventh Wind flared behind him — silent, brilliant, terrifying.

The Tempestborn whispered:

"Then you are my enemy."

Thunder split the sky.

3 "STORMBORN OATHBREAKER"

Perspective: The Tempestborn

Location: Stormcradle Fortress, Tempest Territory

The storm would not obey him.

For the first time in centuries, the Tempestborn stood on the balcony of Stormcradle Fortress and felt the lightning hesitate as it crackled around his armor.

It shivered. It flickered. It resisted.

Because of him.

The Seventh Wind.

Kaelen.

The boy he had once ignored, then feared, then sworn to destroy before the world learned what he truly was.

Lightning stabbed the sky, but the thunder came late — off rhythm — wrong.

The storm was breaking.

Just as it had the first time.

Just as it had when the Tempestborn failed.

He closed his eyes.

He saw the old memory whether he wanted to or not.

I. The Past: The First Storm War

The battlefield had been endless lightning, endless screaming, endless wind collapsing under its own hatred.

And he — the Stormlord of that age — had been at the center of it.

Young.

Proud.

Invincible.

Or so he believed.

He raised his stormblade then, just as he did earlier that day, and hurled himself against the sixth wind.

But the death-wind did not fight him.

It ignored him.

It swallowed entire battalions, erased clans, devoured winds—

yet it passed over the Tempestborn like he didn't matter.

He remembered the shame more than the terror.

He remembered watching his storms fail.

He remembered the Nameless One trying his forbidden ritual.

He remembered sealing the death-wind into the monolith—

Not through strength.

But through sacrifice.

His storm-soul, torn in half.

His immortality broken.

His breath fractured forever.

And he remembered the whisper:

"...you are not the one..."

Even now, centuries later, the memory burned.

So when Kaelen rose from the abyss with a wind the death-wind had never recognized before—

The Tempestborn felt the same humiliation return.

But this time, it was worse.

Because this time, the sixth wind did recognize someone.

And it wasn't him.

II. The Present: The Clans Divide

A Tempest guard approached, armor sparking nervously.

"Stormlord... the clans demand council. They insist the Seventh Wind must be bound or killed."

The Tempestborn laughed bitterly.

"So they finally fear him."

The guard hesitated.

"There are... divisions."

Of course there were.

Sirocco

Half their warriors believed Kaelen was the savior of the world.

The other half feared the drought-winds were responding to him.

Mistral

Some knelt to his balanced breath.

Others swore he was the perfect target for a second erasure ritual.

Zephyr

Half wanted to follow Kaelen because he stabilized their fractured steps.

Half wanted him dead because he stabilized their fractured steps.

Black Wisper

They accepted him entirely.

Silence was loyal.

Tempest

His own clan...

His own warriors...

Some whispered treason.

Some whispered hope.

Some whispered that the Seventh Wind was the true successor of the Primordial Storm and that the Tempestborn was an outdated remnant.

He clenched his fist.

Stormbreaker Fang crackled in response.

"I am still the storm," he growled.

But even he didn't believe it.

III. The Death-Wind Reacts to Kaelen

Thunder faltered.

A cold wind swept into the fortress — not frost, not heat, not silence, not storm.

A hollow wind.

A wind that should not exist.

The Tempestborn's eyes widened.

"No... not now..."

The death-wind crept through the cracks of the fortress like mist shaped from memory and absence. It coiled around his throne. It touched his armor. It whispered into his bones.

"...finally... balance awakens..."

He snarled.

"Stay away from me."

"...you hunted the seventh wind..."

"I will kill him if I must."

"...you cannot..."

Lightning exploded from his armor.

"Why? Because he is favored by you? Because he carries your fragment? Because he—"

The death-wind cut him off with a single echo:

"...because he is what you failed to become..."

The Tempestborn's breath caught.

His storm flickered.

Thunder cracked weakly.

"No..." he whispered. "No, I was chosen. I was forged."

"...he is born..."

The death-wind retreated, leaving frost-cracks on the stone.

The Tempestborn fell to one knee, trembling in rage and despair.

He was no longer the apex wind.

He was no longer the inevitable force.

He was no longer the storm that terrified creation.

He was the Oathbreaker —
the storm that failed twice.

IV. Kaelen's First True Seventh Wind Ability

Far away, Kaelen stood on a ruined cliff with the Unheard, the Scorched Sovereign, and a handful of Zephyr scouts watching him nervously.

Kaelen inhaled.

Wind spiraled around him in perfect harmony.

He exhaled.

A gust rippled outward—

not destructive

not offensive

not defensive

—but equalizing.

Snow melted without heat.

Lightning dissipated without grounding.

Frost softened without losing form.

Heatwaves cooled without dying.

Zephyr flickers stabilized instantly.

Black Wisper silence deepened into clarity.

This was the first named technique of the Seventh Wind:

Equalis: The Breath That Levels All Winds."

The Unheard whispered in awe:

"It restores balance... to everything."

Kaelen opened his eyes.

"I didn't mean to."

"You didn't have to," the Unheard said. "Balance isn't a technique. It's who you've become."

V. The Clans Feel the Shift

Across the continent, the equalizing breath rippled:
Sirocco winds stopped their drought cycle.
Mistral blizzards calmed into controlled frost.
Zephyr forests straightened their broken angles.
Tempest storms weakened.
Black Wisper caverns resonated with perfect silence.
Fear spread faster than wind.
"What is he becoming?"
"Is he rewriting the world?"
"Is he a wind... or a god?"
"Can he erase the clans without violence?"
"Is this balance... or domination?"
Armies mobilized.
Councils fractured.
New alliances formed.
Old hatreds reawakened.
The Seventh Wind was not something they could fight.
He was something they had to survive.

VI. The Tempestborn Makes His Decision

In Stormcradle Fortress, lightning crawled over the Tempest-born's armor.
His breath was uneven.
His storm was unstable.
His pride was shattered.
He rose slowly.
"Prepare the full Tempest Army."
The guard hesitated.
"But the equalizing breath weakened our storm-sense. We cannot—"
The Tempestborn seized him by the throat.

"We march," he snarled.
"Because if I do nothing, the world will forget the storm entirely."

He released the guard, who fled.

The Tempestborn stepped out into the open sky.

Thunder surged as he screamed into the wind:

"SEVENTH WIND! I COME FOR YOU!"

Lightning split the heavens.

Stormbirth flared around him.

And for the first time, the storm trembled.

Not out of weakness—

but because it feared the wind that was no longer a storm.

4 "THE GATHERING TEMPEST"
Location: The Whispered Plateau
Temporary Refuge of the Seventh Wind

The world hummed.
Not with wind.
Not with storm.
Not with battle.
With fear.
Wind itself carried it — thin currents of panic drifting across the continent like smoke from an unseen fire.
Kaelen stood at the cliff edge, eyes closed, letting the winds speak for themselves.
Sirocco gusts carried doubt.
Zephyr breezes carried confusion.
Mistral drafts carried condemnation.
Tempest gales carried rage.
Even Black Wisper silence vibrated with unease.
They were afraid of him.
"You hear it, don't you?" the Unheard said softly behind him.
Kaelen nodded.
"They think I'm a threat."
"They are wind-born clans," the Unheard replied. "And you have become something that rewrites wind."
Kaelen clenched his fists.
"I didn't ask for this."
"No wind chooses how it is born," the Unheard said. "Only how it moves."
Kaelen opened his eyes.
Far across the horizon, thunder rolled.

Stormcradle Fortress.

The Tempestborn was mobilizing.

And the winds trembled with anticipation.

The storm was gathering.

I. The Clans Convene in Secret

Zephyr scouts flickered into view beside Kaelen.

"Three clans are calling a covert council," said the first scout. "Mistral, Sirocco, and half of Zephyr."

"And Tempest?" Kaelen asked.

"They prepare for war," said the second scout.

"And Black Wisper?" Kaelen asked, already knowing.

The Unheard answered.

"We stand with you."

Kaelen's jaw tightened.

"They all think I'll destroy the world."

The Unheard shook his head.

"No. They fear you will change it."

Kaelen felt a chill.

"Is that worse?"

"Always," the Unheard whispered.

I. The Secret Third Prophecy

The wind shifted suddenly.

Cold.

Sharp.

Awake.

Kaelen inhaled—

—and the world vanished.

Instead of cliffs, he stood in a void of pale white wind.

A place between breaths, between thoughts, between futures.

A voice spoke:

"...listener..."

The Remembering Current manifested, glowing softly.

"...the clans know two prophecies...

...but you must hear the third...

...the one meant only for the Seventh Wind..."

Kaelen steadied himself.

"I'm listening."

Wind rippled.

Symbols formed around him in spirals of ancient breath — runes older than the clans, older than the Primordial Winds, older than even the first storm.

The Third Prophecy unfolded as a whisper layered through silence:

*THE **3rd** PROPHECY*

(Heard ONLY by Kaelen)

"When balance awakens,
the storm will recoil.
When harmony breathes,
the world will divide.

When six winds tremble,
a seventh shall rise.
Not to conquer,
not to erase.

But to reveal.

For in the age of broken breath,
truth itself is the first casualty.
And only the Seventh Wind
can separate truth from lie,
memory from illusion,
destiny from deceit.

If he accepts this burden,
the world will finally see.
If he rejects it,
the unbreath will feast.

And if he hesitates—
the stormborn oathbreaker
shall drown the world in thunder."

The prophecy shattered into light.

Kaelen fell back onto the cliff, gasping.

The Unheard rushed to his side.

"What did you see?"

Kaelen's hands trembled.

"The truth," he whispered.

"And the lies."

III. Kaelen's Second Ability — Divisio

"Divisio — The Breath That Separates Truth From Lie."

Kaelen stood slowly and looked at the Unheard.

"Something's... changed," he whispered.

"How?" the Unheard asked cautiously.

Kaelen inhaled — not deeply, not forcefully.

A soft, spiraling wind formed around him.

He exhaled gently toward the ground.

A single gust formed—

—and the air split into two currents:

one warm and bright

one cold and trembling

Kaelen blinked.

He stepped toward the cold current.

Visions flickered in it:

The Tempestborn practicing secret erasure-resistant storm forms

The Mistral planning a second forbidden ritual

Zephyr factions debating assassination

The Scorched Sovereign whispering fears of Kaelen's power

Black Wisper spies shadowing the Tempestborn

The death-wind awakening deeper underground

And something else—

something older

something watching

Kaelen stumbled back.

"What... was that?"

The Unheard stared in awe.

"You split reality's breath.
You revealed truth... and unveiled secrets."

Kaelen took a shaky breath.

"So this is the Seventh Wind."

"No," said the Unheard. "This is only the beginning."

IV. The Death-Wind Evolves

A hollow wind rolled across the plateau.

Kaelen stiffened.

The Unheard stepped back.

Zephyr scouts vanished in fear.

Sirocco heat faltered.

The wind was familiar—
and different.

The death-wind rose from the canyon base, swirling upward
like a dark cyclone of unbreath and fractured memory.

But now—
it had shape.

A humanoid silhouette formed within the vortex.

Not solid.

Not stable.

But present.

It was learning form.

Kaelen gasped.

"It's... evolving."

The silhouette tilted its head.

Its voice split in two —
one tone ancient and hollow,
the other disturbingly close to a human whisper:

"...seventh wind...
...you changed the balance...
...so I must change as well..."

Kaelen stepped forward.

"What do you want?"

The death-wind pulsed.

"...to finish what was begun..."

"Erasure?" Kaelen asked.

"...balance..."

"Balance through destruction?"

"...balance through truth..."

The Unheard whispered urgently:

"Kaelen... it has sensed your second ability."

The death-wind continued:

"...you see truth now...

...soon you will see the truth of me..."

Kaelen's breath tightened.

"What truth?"

The wind twisted, forming a mockery of a smile.

"...that I am not your enemy...

...but your shadow...

...and when you rise,

I rise with you..."

The wind dissolved into nothing.

Kaelen staggered.

His shadow flickered unnaturally behind him.

The Unheard placed a hand on his shoulder.

"Kaelen," he whispered, "what did it mean?"

Kaelen's eyes focused on the horizon where thunder gathered.

"It means," Kaelen said quietly, "that every time I grow stronger...

the death-wind grows stronger too."

The wind fell still.

The world held its breath.

The Tempestborn's storm loomed closer.

The age of balance had begun.
The age of reckoning followed.

5 "CONCLAVE OF THE BROKEN WINDS"
Location: The Whispered Plateau
Now Neutral Ground by Force
All Five Clans Called to Council.

The Seventh Wind Summoned by Storm.
Thunder rolled.
Frost crawled.
Heat shimmered.
Silence deepened.
Flickers scattered.

The skies above the Whispered Plateau churned with every clan's breath — a storm of divided loyalties and growing panic.

The Conclave was assembling.

Not by choice.

By fear.

At the edge of the plateau stood Kaelen, the Seventh Wind, flanked only by the Unheard and the Fragmented Master. Zephyr scouts flickered nervously around them.

Kaelen inhaled.

Wind bent.

Fear rose like dust.

He exhaled.

Silence spread through the plateau — not Wisper-silence, not death-wind silence —

A balancing silence.

The Seventh Wind commanding the air to listen.

The clans arrived.

I. The Five Clans Arrive in Fractured Force

Sirocco marched with heat-shields raised, wary of both Tempest lightning and Kaelen's equalizing breath.

Mistral descended with frost-masks, their eyes unreadable, their loyalty divided.

Zephyr flickered in fractured battalions, some ready to join Kaelen, others ready to strike.

Black Wisper materialized without sound, forming a protective crescent behind Kaelen.

Tempest marched last, their storm so heavy that clouds bent around their army.

Lightning cracked as the Tempestborn's armored boots touched the plateau.

His storm pressed down on Kaelen like a weight of judgment.

Kaelen felt the pressure —
but only for a moment.

The Seventh Wind pressed back.

And the storm strained against him.

The Tempestborn noticed.

His rage grew.

But the Conclave began.

II. Kaelen Confronts the Clans

The Scorched Sovereign stepped forward first.

"Seventh Wind," she said carefully, "you've altered the world's breath. Even Sirocco's drought-winds obey your call. How far does your influence reach?"

Kaelen resisted the urge to retreat.

"I don't influence. I stabilize."

Mistral's frozen envoy hissed, "Then why does the world tremble? Why do blizzards distort? Why do memories shift?"

Kaelen looked down.

"Because balance forces truth into the open."

Zephyr's leader flickered around Kaelen.

"And truth frightens the clans more than war."

Black Wisper remained still.

The Tempestborn stepped into the gap.

"Seventh Wind. Kaelen. Listener," he said mockingly. "You stand before the clans. Tell us plainly:
What are you?"

Kaelen inhaled.

The wind rippled.

He exhaled.

"I am what the Primordial Winds created and what the death-wind lost."

Silence.

Shock.

Fear.

The Scorched Sovereign's voice wavered.
"You speak of the Primordial Winds as if they still exist."
"They do," Kaelen said. "And they warned me."
Mistral's envoy snapped, "Warned you of what?"
Kaelen looked directly at the Tempestborn.
"Of the storm preparing to break the world."
The plateau erupted into shouting.
Zephyr flickers flared.
Sirocco heat pulsed.
Mistral frost crackled.
The Tempestborn raised his blade, storming forward.
"You dare accuse me—"
Kaelen raised his hand.
And the storm bent around him.
The Tempestborn froze.
Because Kaelen had not used Equalis.
He had used something else.

III. Kaelen's Third Ability — Sunder

"Sunder — The Breath That Breaks Fate."
Kaelen inhaled a thin strand of wind — nothing more than a whisper.
He exhaled.
A thin line of shimmering energy split the air.
It moved like a blade made of wind—
but it wasn't cutting flesh.
It was cutting future.
Reality trembled.
The ground beneath the Tempestborn cracked, splitting in a perfect arc before him — as if Kaelen had severed the path the Tempestborn was about to walk.
Kaelen whispered:
"Sunder breaks the momentum of fate.
It severs intention from outcome."

The Tempestborn staggered backward.

"What... what have you become?"

Kaelen lowered his hand.

"Someone who won't let you destroy the world again."

The Tempestborn's storm flared violently.

Thunder cracked so loud the plateau shook.

The clans watched in horrified fascination.

The Seventh Wind had not attacked.

Had not harmed.

Had not dominated.

He had broken fate.

That terrified them more than any battle technique.

IV. Tempestborn POV — Preparing the World-Ending Storm

Location: The Eye of the Tempest — His Inner Storm

The Tempestborn retreated into his mind, into the storm that had fueled him for centuries.

But now—

It was unstable.

Lightning stuttered.

Clouds dissipated.

Thunder broke rhythm.

The Seventh Wind had shaken the foundation of the storm.

He roared into the void.

"I AM THE STORM!

I AM THE FATE OF THE CLANS!

I DO NOT FALL TO BALANCE!"

But a whisper echoed through the storm:

"...you already have..."

His own breath betrayed him.

The death-wind had said the same thing.

And now Kaelen had shown him why.

The Seventh Wind wasn't just powerful.

He was inevitable.

Unless—

Unless the Tempestborn unleashed the technique he swore never to use again.

Storm's Ending.
A world-ending wind.
A storm born from sacrificing what remained of his storm-soul.
It would cost him everything.
But it might kill the Seventh Wind.
He opened his eyes.
Thunder trembled.
"So be it."

V. The Death-Wind Evolves — Identity Mimicry

Back on the plateau, a cold wind crawled up Kaelen's spine.
He turned.
A whisper rose.
Not chaotic.
Not hollow.
But familiar.
A silhouette formed in the dusty wind—
and its shape was Kaelen's.
Exactly. Perfectly.
Not a shadow.
Not an illusion.
A duplicate.
The death-wind spoke in his voice:
"Balance births reflection.
I reflect you now."
Kaelen froze.
The Unheard stepped forward, horrified.
"It has learned... identity."
Mistral warriors stumbled backward.
"That is impossible—unbreath cannot hold form!"
Zephyr flickered in terror.
Sirocco heat extinguished.
The Tempestborn watched with a mix of awe and hatred.
The death-wind Kaelen smiled with no warmth.

"...I evolve as you evolve...
When you breathe truth, I breathe deception...
When you cut fate, I cut identity...
When you become wind...
...I become storm AND silence..."

Kaelen felt the abyss inside his chest tighten.

"What are you becoming?"

The death-wind tilted its head — Kaelen's head.

"...your opposite...
your mirror...
your necessary end..."

The real Kaelen whispered:

"My shadow..."

The death-wind echoed:

"...your undoing."

The death-wind duplicate dissolved into swirling absence.

The plateau shook.

The clans trembled.

Kaelen understood:

Every ability he gained
Every breath he learned
Every truth he revealed

—the death-wind would mimic, distort, weaponize.

The Seventh Wind had awakened.

So had its anti-wind.

Balance demanded it.

Fate screamed it.

War promised it.

6   "THE STORM'S FIRST VICTIM"
Location: The Whispered Plateau
The Tempest Barrens

Moments after the death-wind duplicate vanishes...

A silence fell across the Conclave.

Not the silence of the Wisper.

Not the silence of terror.

But the silence of fate tightening its grip.

Kaelen stared at the place where his death-wind reflection had stood.

"It's learning faster than I expected," he whispered.

The Unheard nodded solemnly.

"It learns because you learn. You evolve, it evolves. You balance, it breaks."

Mistral's envoy shivered.

"This world cannot survive two K–Kaelens."

The Zephyr leader flickered in panic.

"No world can."

Sirocco warriors tightened their ranks.

And then—

The sky turned black.

Not clouded.

Not stormed.

Blotted out.

Thunder cracked across the horizon with a force that rattled bones.

Lightning spiraled downward in unnatural, spiraling patterns — intentional, deliberate.

A storm was forming.

A forbidden storm.

Kaelen's breath hitched.

"He's doing it," he whispered.

"He's using Storm's Ending."

The Unheard turned sharply.

"No... he wouldn't—"

But he would.

He had.

The Tempestborn was unleashing the storm that was forbidden even in the First War.

A storm built from sacrifice.

A storm built from half a soul.

A storm that did not stop until it erased everything in its path.

A world-ender.

I. Tempestborn POV — Storm's Ending Begins

Location: The Eye of the Stormborn's Mind

He knelt at the center of the cyclone he had summoned.

Lightning spiraled around him like the rings of a dying star.

His breath shook.

His heartbeat fractured.

His storm-soul flickered like a failing flame.

"This world fears the Seventh Wind...

but it has forgotten the Stormlord."

He drove Stormbreaker Fang into the ground.

It pierced the world.

The earth cracked.

Thunder screamed.

Clouds descended.

The storm obeyed.

But his own mind...

began to break.

He whispered through blood:

"Let the Seventh Wind face a world without balance."

And the storm answered.

II. The Storm Hits — The First Victim

Back on the plateau, a bolt of lightning thicker than a tree struck the ground with a deafening roar.

A Zephyr scout screamed—

And vanished.

Not burned.

Not shattered.

Erased by lightning.

Kaelen staggered backward.

"He didn't just strike him—he removed him from the wind."

Sirocco shields flared.

Black Wisper attempted to dampen the sound.

Mistral frost raced to counter the heat.

Zephyr flickers failed to dodge.

The storm grew.

The sky tore open.

And then—

The death-wind Kaelen reappeared.

It formed from the lightning itself, stepping out of a spiral of unlight.

Its voice was quiet. Calm.

"...the first storm creates the first shadow..."

It raised a hand.

Wind bent around it—

not like Kaelen's balance,

but like a mockery of fate.

A Sirocco warrior rushed too close.

The death-wind Kaelen exhaled.

Just one breath.

A whisper.

A distortion.

And the warrior's shadow detached—
stepped away—
and took the warrior with it.
The man was gone.
The death-wind Kaelen tilted its head and smiled.
"...one truth removed..."
The Conclave collapsed into terror.

II. Kaelen Awakens Resonantia

"The Breath That Hears Every Wind"

Lightning screamed overhead.

Death-wind whispered at his back.

Clans shouted.

Wind bent.

Balance trembled.

Kaelen collapsed to one knee, pressing a hand to the ground.

The winds were screaming.

Too many voices.

Too many lies.

Too many truths.

Too much storm.

Too much unbreath.

He gasped.

"I... I can't hear them all—"

The Unheard grabbed his shoulders.

"You are the Seventh Wind.

You were born to hear what others fear."

Kaelen closed his eyes.

He inhaled.

And the world fell silent.

Absolute silence.

Then—

He heard them.

All at once.

Every wind.
Every clan.
Every fear.
Every lie.
Every intention.
Every storm.
Every draft.
Every whisper.
Every cry.
His heart nearly burst from the pressure.
But he held on.
Wind spiraled around him in seven layers of motion.
His eyes opened—
and wind radiated outward from his irises.
The winds spoke to him:
Sirocco fear
Zephyr fractured truth
Mistral hidden plans
Tempestborn's collapsing soul
Black Wisper's silent warnings
Death-wind Kaelen's growing hunger
This was Resonantia — The Breath That Hears Every Wind.
Kaelen whispered:
"I hear all of you."
And with that hearing came clarity.

IV. Storm's Ending — The World Beginning to Crack

Kaelen looked to the horizon.
The forbidden storm rose like a titanic wall of lightning and thunder.
It was pulling wind—ALL wind—into itself:
Sirocco heat
Mistral frost

Zephyr motion

Black Wisper silence

Even death-wind absence

It was devouring the world's breath.

Kaelen gasped.

"He's trying to erase the winds themselves."

The Unheard stiffened.

"That storm will consume entire continents. It cannot end until the Tempestborn's soul is gone."

Kaelen trembled.

"Then we must stop him."

Zephyr flickered forward.

"How? No wind can break Storm's Ending."

Kaelen looked at his hands.

"Maybe not a wind."

He inhaled.

Seven winds responded.

He exhaled.

Balance formed around him.

"I'm not just a wind anymore."

V. The Death-Wind Kaelen Begins Its Hunt

Lightning struck the plateau again.

The death-wind Kaelen stepped out of the blast, eyes glowing with voidlight.

It looked at Kaelen.

Not with hatred.

Not with anger.

With inevitability.

"...as the storm breaks, the shadow hunts..."

It flickered once.

Twice.

Then it vanished.

Not into wind.
Not into silence.
Into identity.
Kaelen felt a cold shiver.
"It can walk memories.
It can walk truths.
It can walk lies."
The Unheard whispered:
"It can walk you."
Kaelen staggered back.
"How do I fight something that can become me?"
The world trembled.
The storm roared.
The death-wind whispered inside his bones:
"...you don't..."
The Unheard grabbed Kaelen's arm.
"Then learn how."
Kaelen looked at the coming storm.
"I will."

7 "INTO THE FORBIDDEN STORM"
Location: Approaching the Tempest Barrens

Entering Storm's Ending

The world trembled like a dying animal.

Storm's Ending blanketed the horizon—a wall of lightning spirals, thunder implosions, clouds twisted into shapes that defied nature.

It was not weather.

It was erasure wearing the costume of a storm.

Kaelen stood at the edge of the devastation, cloak snapping violently in the unstable wind.

The Unheard hovered behind him.

"This storm will unmake you," he warned.

"Then I have to be something it cannot unmake," Kaelen replied.

He inhaled.

Seven winds answered.

He exhaled.

The ground stabilized under his feet.

And he stepped into the storm.

I. Inside Storm's Ending — The Storm That Devours Destiny

The moment Kaelen crossed the threshold, reality bent.

Lightning moved in reverse.

Thunder rolled silently.

Raindrops rose upward into the sky.

Shadows fell in the wrong direction.

Wind spiraled around him—not flowing, but feeding.

Not a storm.

A hunger.

Kaelen pressed forward, every breath a battle.

He could feel the Tempestborn's presence like a colossal heartbeat pulsing through the clouds.

Ba-dum.

Storm crackled.

Ba-dum.

Light bent.

Ba-dum.

Reality shook.

Kaelen whispered:

"He is using his own soul as fuel…"

The Unheard's voice echoed faintly through the chaos:

"The longer Storm's Ending lives, the more of him dies."

Kaelen moved deeper.

The air grew thick with memories that weren't his:

The First Storm War

The Tempestborn kneeling in defeat

The death-wind ignoring him

The shame of being unchosen

The agony of splitting his soul

The prophecy he hid from all clans

Kaelen stumbled.

These weren't hallucinations.

Storm's Ending was showing him the Tempestborn's fate.

And then he saw him.

II. The Tempestborn — Half Man, Half Storm

At the center of the cyclone floated the Tempestborn.

Or what remained of him.

Lightning veined through his body.

His armor had fused with cloud and thunder.

His eyes burned with crackling storms.

His breath was ragged.

His voice echoed like thunder splitting mountains.

"You came," he said.

Kaelen stepped forward, wind swirling around him.

"Stop the storm. You'll destroy the world."

The Tempestborn laughed, a sound like shattering stone.

"That is the idea."

Kaelen shook his head.

"You're dying."

"Dying?" the Tempestborn thundered.

"No. I am ascending."

The storm flared around him.

"I was denied becoming the Seventh Wind.

I was denied my destiny.

But I will not be denied the right to end this broken world."

Kaelen braced as a lightning arc split the ground.

"Why?" Kaelen shouted.

"Why destroy everything?"

The Tempestborn's eyes flashed with ancient pain.

"Because the storm was never meant to kneel to balance.

And now that you exist...

all storms must."

Kaelen exhaled slowly.

"I'm not your jailer."

"You are my replacement."

The cyclone tightened around them.

"You are the Seventh Wind.

And I am the storm that breaks before the seventh breath.

It is fate."

Kaelen's eyes hardened.

"Then I'll break fate."

III. Kaelen Awakens His 5th Ability

"Concordia — The Breath That Unifies"

The storm's pressure became unbearable.

Kaelen couldn't breathe.

He couldn't move.

His wind shattered—

and the death-wind flickered inside him.

He felt both winds tearing at his lungs.

He dropped to one knee.

"This is it..." Kaelen whispered. "I can't... I can't fight both..."

The Unheard's voice whispered in his mind:

"You don't fight them.

You unify them."

Kaelen closed his eyes.

He inhaled.

Hard.

Pain flooded his body as storm, silence, heat, frost, fragment, and unbreath slammed into him.

Then—

He exhaled.

And something impossible happened.

The winds merged.

Not blended.

Not dominated.

Not suppressed.

Unified.

The storm stopped shrinking.

The silence stopped consuming.

The frost stopped fracturing.

The heat stopped burning.

The fragment stopped flickering.

The unbreath stopped erasing.

Kaelen whispered the name:

"Concordia."

Thunder collapsed into harmony.

Kaelen rose.

His eyes glowed with unified wind.

The Seventh Wind had finally become whole.

Even the Tempestborn froze.

"What... what have you done?"

Kaelen stepped forward.

"I am not a wind.

I am all winds."

IV. The Tempestborn Breaks

For the first time since the First War, the Tempestborn felt fear.

"You... unified wind? Impossible."

Kaelen raised his hand.

Storm-soul energy came loose from the Tempestborn's body.

He screamed as lightning bled out of him.

"Stop! STOP!"

Kaelen whispered:

"No one else dies because of your storm."

He placed a hand on the Tempestborn's chest.

Wind unified between them.

Storm unraveled.

The Tempestborn fell—

not dead,

but broken beyond pride.

Kaelen caught him.

"You're not my enemy," Kaelen said softly. "You never were."

The Tempestborn whispered, tears mixing with storm-water:

"I just... wanted to matter."

Kaelen nodded.

"You do."

The storm collapsed.

V. The Death-Wind Kaelen Begins Stealing Identities

Back on the plateau, warriors sought shelter from fading lightning.

A Mistral scout ran into the camp, exhausted.

"Help!" she cried. "He—he won't stop!"

They rushed toward her—

And the Unheard froze.

Her breath.

Her wind.

Her shadow.

None of it matched.

Identity mismatch.

He whispered:

"Kaelen... that's not her."

The scout smiled darkly.

Her face flickered—

and changed.

Into a Sirocco warrior.

Then a Zephyr scout.

Then a Tempest soldier.

Then a Wisper shade.

Then—

Kaelen.

Perfectly.

The death-wind Kaelen laughed softly.

"...shadow becomes face...

face becomes truth...

truth becomes prey..."

It stepped into the Mistral ranks—

and several Mistral warriors vanished into shadow.

The clans screamed.

The death-wind Kaelen whispered:

"...I hunt identity...
I wear identity...
I erase identity..."
The war had changed.
And the death-wind was done waiting.

8
"THE SHADOW THAT WEARS THE WIND"
Location: Whispered Plateau
Minutes After the Collapse of Storm's Ending

The storm died.

Silence did not follow.

Instead, chaos erupted.

Mistral warriors stabbed at Sirocco warriors, claiming their shadows had moved wrong.

Zephyr flickers fought their own reflections, unable to tell which were real.

Sirocco flames erupted in blind panic.

Tempest soldiers roared, demanding Kaelen reveal every infiltrator.

Black Wisper assassins vanished into the fog, hunting the unseen enemy.

The Conclave shattered.

Wind became war.

Kaelen emerged from the fading storm-wall carrying the unconscious Tempestborn.

The clans froze.

Sirocco gasped.

Mistral recoiled.

Zephyr flickered in disbelief.

Tempest warriors dropped to one knee.

Wisper shades bowed.

The Scorched Sovereign whispered:

"You... neutralized Storm's Ending?"

Kaelen nodded slowly.

But before anyone could speak—
a scream tore across the plateau.
A Zephyr scout shouted:
"HE TOOK HER FACE! HE TOOK HER FACE!"
Kaelen felt the air shift.
Cold.
Hollow.
Wrong.
He turned.
And there it was.

I. The Death-Wind Kaelen Appears

It stepped calmly out of a swirl of dark wind.
A perfect copy of Kaelen.
Eyes glowing faintly with unbreath.
Breath silent.
Presence empty.
Shadow independent.
It smiled gently — Kaelen's smile, but wrong.
"...balance breathes...
shadow follows..."
The clans backed away in horror.
Sirocco spears raised.
Mistral frost surged.
Zephyr flickers encircled.
Tempest lightning gathered.
Black Wisper shadows sharpened.
The death-wind Kaelen spoke softly:
"...war suits you better than peace..."
Then it moved.
Faster than Zephyr.
Colder than Mistral.
Hotter than Sirocco.

Louder than Tempest.

Quieter than Wisper.

A perfect hybrid of all winds—

a mockery of the Seventh.

It stepped between two Tempest soldiers.

Both vanished without a cry.

It looked at the crowd:

"...identity is fragile..."

"...allow me to break it..."

Kaelen stepped forward.

"STOP!"

The death-wind Kaelen turned toward him, head tilting.

"...you have grown..."

"I'm not your enemy."

"...no...

you are my path..."

It stepped closer.

"And I am your mirror."

II. Kaelen vs. the Shadow — First Confrontation

Kaelen braced.

Wind swirled behind him — all seven currents merging in a controlled harmony.

His reflection stood before him — seven winds broken, corrupted, inverted.

They circled each other.

Two images.

Two destinies.

Two breaths of the same wind.

Kaelen spoke first.

"You don't have to be this."

The death-wind Kaelen smiled.

"...I am what you deny..."

Kaelen inhaled — Resonantia activating.

He felt:

Sirocco panic

Mistral fury

Zephyr confusion

Tempest hatred

Wisper dread

Unbreath hunger

He staggered under the weight.

The death-wind spoke:

"...you hear too much...

...it will break you..."

Kaelen gritted his teeth.

"No. It will guide me."

He exhaled.

Concordia.

The seven winds aligned around him, forming a unified barrier.

The death-wind Kaelen's smile dropped.

"...unity...

...unnatural..."

It lunged.

Kaelen met the strike.

Wind exploded.

Lightning spiraled.

Frost shattered.

Heat warped.

Silence howled.

Fragments flickered.

Unbreath devoured light.

Both Kaelens were thrown back.

Kaelen slid across the stone.

His double landed silently, unharmed.

"...you unify...

...I divide..."

Its shadow stretched unnaturally toward a group of warriors.

Kaelen gasped.

"NO!"

He launched forward—

But too late.

The Mistral envoy's breath was torn from his body, leaving him standing hollow-eyed—alive, but emptied.

Sirocco shields flared, trying to contain the panic.

Tempest warriors charged at the wrong enemies.

Zephyr flickered in desperate arcs.

Black Wisper tried to form a silence-field—
But their own shadows betrayed them.
Clans turned on clans.
Clans turned on themselves.
Wind became massacre.
The death-wind Kaelen spread its arms.
"...chaos is clarity..."
Kaelen shouted:
"STOP HURTING THEM!"
The shadow turned.
"...then stop me..."

II. Kaelen Tries Resonantia — And Fails

Kaelen inhaled.

Resonantia flared—he heard every breath, every fear, every lie on the battlefield.

It overwhelmed him.

There were too many voices.

Too many truths.

Too many identities.

Too many lies.

He staggered to one knee.

His reflection smiled.

"...you cannot hear what does not wish to be heard..."

Kaelen clutched his chest.

The death-wind Kaelen whispered:

"...you unify...

...I unmake..."

A Zephyr warrior screamed as her shadow peeled away.

Kaelen felt the wind collapsing.

He tried to stand.

But his double pressed a hand to the air—and wind obeyed it.

Kaelen fell again.

"Why... are you doing this?"

The death-wind Kaelen leaned close.

He whispered into Kaelen's ear with Kaelen's voice:

"...because you are balance...
...and I am what balance fears..."

IV. The Clans Turn on Each Other

The breaking point finally arrived.

A Tempest soldier stabbed a Mistral warrior, convinced he was the impostor.

A Zephyr flicker stabbed a Zephyr flicker, unable to tell who was real.

A Sirocco warrior burned a Wisper shade, believing the silence was masking mimicry.

The plateau became a battlefield of confusion.

Identity had become a liability.

Wind became weapon.

The Scorched Sovereign screamed:

"STOP! WE ARE KILLING OUR OWN!"

But no one knew who "our own" was anymore.

Kaelen looked around in horror.

"This is what you want?" he shouted at his shadow.

The death-wind Kaelen smiled.

"...no...
this is what they do...
when truth is taken..."

It spread its arms.

"...and I simply take it."

V. Kaelen Stands — The Seventh Wind Refuses to Break

Blood and wind soaked the battlefield.

Panic clawed at Kaelen's lungs.

His reflection's voice whispered in his mind:

"...you cannot stop what you cannot define..."

Kaelen clenched his fists.

"I won't let you win."

His double tilted its head.

"...you already are..."
Kaelen rose — slowly, painfully — but with unbroken resolve.
Seven winds spiraled around him again.
Unification pulsed.
Balance returned.
The Seventh Wind awakened fully.
Kaelen whispered:
"Then I define you now."
His double froze for the first time.
Kaelen stepped forward, eyes glowing.
"You are not me."
Wind trembled.
"You are not truth."
Thunder cracked.
"You are not balance."
Frost shattered.
"You are the shadow that fears the light."
Unbreath faltered.
Kaelen raised his hand.
Wind gathered behind him like wings.
"And I will break you."
The death-wind Kaelen narrowed its eyes.
For the first time—
it looked afraid.
"...interesting..."
The winds howled.
War paused.
Two destinies faced each other.
And the world waited for the next breath.

9 "THE FRACTURED ARMY"
Location: Whispered Plateau
Now a Battlefield of Uncertainty

W ind howled.
Flames spiraled.
Frost split stone.
Lightning tore the sky.
Shadows cut through breath.
Fragments blurred reality.

The Conclave was gone.

In its place:
War without sides.
War without certainty.
War without identity.

Kaelen stood at the center, breathing hard, bloodied from the previous clash with his shadow. The Unheard hovered beside him, equally shaken.

All around them, the clans tore each other apart.

I. The Clans Fall into Civil War

Sirocco vs. Sirocco

Two Sirocco captains clashed violently — each claiming the other was shadow-wrought. Heatwaves collided, burning the sand into glass.

Zephyr vs. Zephyr

Flicker-steps moved in mirrored chaos, each thinking they fought an imposter. Broken-motion made truth impossible to see.

Mistral vs. Tempest

Mistral frost shields clashed with Tempest lightning as soldiers believed the other side had been entirely infiltrated.

Black Wisper vs. Everyone

Wisper silence spread across the plateau, but the clans interpreted it as mimicry — believing the Wisper hid stolen identities.

Tempest vs. Themselves

Some believed the Tempestborn had fallen.

Some believed Kaelen had possessed him.

Some believed their own shadows were whispering wrong.

No one trusted wind.

No one trusted breath.

No one trusted themselves.

Kaelen inhaled deeply —

And felt the world cracking.

Wind itself was breaking apart.

II. The Shadow Kaelen Escalates Identity Theft

The death-wind Kaelen appeared again.

But not as Kaelen.

This time it wore:

A Sirocco captain's face

A Zephyr scout's breath

A Tempest lieutenant's storm

A Mistral elder's gait

A Wisper assassin's silence

It flickered between them like a nightmare taking inventory.

It approached a group of warriors locked in a stalemate.

"Which of you is real?" one Zephyr cried.

The shadow smiled with a borrowed face.

"...none..."

It placed its hand on the air.

Wind folded.

Four warriors vanished without screams —
reduced to broken shadows absorbed into the Unbreath mimic.
It whispered:
"...identity is a door...
...and I walk freely..."
Kaelen felt his breath seize.
"How do I stop something that can become anyone?"
The Unheard whispered:
"You don't. Not yet."

III. Kaelen Tries to Impose Unity

Kaelen stepped forward.
He inhaled.
The plateau trembled.
He exhaled his power:
Concordia — The Breath That Unifies
Seven winds surged outward in a shimmering wave.
Heat softened.
Frost melted.
Lightning calmed.
Silence steadied.
Fragment stabilized.
Wind aligned.
And for one moment—
the battlefield paused.
Warriors lowered weapons.
Shadows retreated.
Wind exhaled.
Kaelen shouted:
"STOP!
You are fighting illusions and shadows — not each other!"
A Sirocco captain shouted back:
"That is what a mimic would say!"
A Mistral elder froze in dread.

"How do we know if you are real?"

Zephyr flickered in panic.

"What if we're already dead? What if we're shadows?"

Tempest soldiers roared:

"SHOW US PROOF!"

Kaelen looked around in horror.

Unity was not enough.

Fear overwrote reason.

And then the death-wind Kaelen whispered in twenty voices:

"...he unifies...

because he fears division..."

Chaos erupted again.

Kaelen fell to his knees.

His breath shook.

"I can't stop them..."

The Unheard placed a hand on his shoulder.

"They don't need a wind right now."

Kaelen looked up, confused.

"They need a leader."

IV. Kaelen Confronts the Battlefield — Alone

Kaelen stood and inhaled slowly.

Resonantia awakened.

The winds of the battlefield spoke:

Sirocco's fear of heat turning against them

Zephyr's fear of never knowing identity again

Mistral's fear of having their memories stolen

Tempest's fear of losing control

Wisper's fear of silence being mistaken for hostility

Kaelen exhaled.

He stepped onto a shattered rock.

Wind gathered around him.

He shouted — not with storm, not with silence, but with unity:

"ENOUGH!"

The winds responded.

But the clans did not.

A Tempest soldier attacked a Sirocco warrior.

A Zephyr flicker stabbed a Mistral captain.

A Wisper assassin killed another Wisper assassin — convinced the other was a mimic.

Kaelen whispered:

"They won't listen…"

The Unheard nodded.

"Fear listens only to itself."

Kaelen clenched his fists.

"Then I need something stronger than unity."

V. The Death-Wind Kaelen Strikes the Heart

The ground cracked.

The shadow Kaelen emerged inside a cluster of overlapping battles.

It looked directly at Kaelen and spoke with Kaelen's voice:

"…you cannot bring unity to those who worship division…"

Then it stabbed its hand into the air.

Wind broke.

Dozens of warriors fell — not dead, but hollow, their identities ripped away and replaced with flickering, empty shadows.

Kaelen screamed:

"STOP!"

His double smiled.

"…why?

Division is your weakness.

And my strength."

It dissolved into a hundred faces—

all stolen.

All perfect.

All lies.

Kaelen shook violently.

He whispered:

"I'm losing them..."

The Unheard leaned close.

"Then stop trying to save the clans."

Kaelen turned to him, confused.

The Unheard whispered:

"Save the wind."

VI. Kaelen Chooses a New Path

Kaelen closed his eyes.

He inhaled.

He exhaled.

Not Concordia.

Not Resonantia.

Not Sunder.

Something deeper.

Balance.

Wind calmed around him, forming a sphere of silence.

He whispered:

"I must unify the wind before I unify the people."

The Unheard nodded.

"And only then can you face the shadow."

Kaelen stood tall — wind swirling like a quiet storm behind him.

His next breath would reshape the war.

His next choice would determine the fate of the clans.

His next step would lead to the confrontation destiny demanded.

He whispered:

"Shadow...

I'm coming for you."

The battlefield trembled.

The death-wind Kaelen turned, feeling the shift.

It smiled.
And vanished.

10

"THE HUNT FOR THE TRUE SELF"

Location: Between Realities
The Memory Corridor

Wind fell silent.

Kaelen stepped into a space that wasn't space.

Not ground.

Not sky.

Not the plateau.

A long corridor of floating, shifting fragments stretched before him — memories suspended like lanterns in a void. Some glowed. Some flickered. Some bled shadow.

This was no place he had ever walked.

This was identity unbound.

And his shadow was somewhere inside it.

The Unheard drifted at his side, silent but tense.

Kaelen whispered:

"Where are we?"

The Unheard answered:

"We are inside the wind's memory.

Where truth, lie, identity, and breath overlap."

Kaelen swallowed hard.

"Why bring me here?"

"To hunt the shadow where it feels strongest."

I. Entering the Memory of the Winds

Kaelen touched the first memory-fragment.

Light erupted.

Suddenly he stood in a forgotten Sirocco desert — a burning wind roaring across ancient dunes. He saw a Sirocco warrior screaming as the death-wind took his shadow centuries ago.

A lie replaced him.

Then the scene broke.

Kaelen stepped into a Zephyr forest, watching flicker-walkers training in fractured steps — then one of them vanished mid-step, another identity eaten by unbreath.

Then the memory shattered.

He found himself in the First Storm War, watching the Tempestborn fail—

watching him fall to his knees as the death-wind ignored him—watching shame carve itself into his soul.

Kaelen tore himself free from the memory, staggering back into the corridor.

"This place..." Kaelen whispered.

"It's showing me everything the death-wind ever touched."

"No," the Unheard said quietly.

"It's showing you everything the wind remembers."

I. The Shadow Leaves Him Clues — Mocking Him

A whisper echoed through the corridor:

"...Kaelen..."

It came from everywhere.

It came from nowhere.

His shadow.

Kaelen ran after the sound, weaving through collapsing memories and drifting shards of vanished lives.

He turned a corner—

And froze.

A memory was projected before him:

His own childhood.

A boy kneeling beside a river, staring at the reflection in the water.

A reflection that did not match his breath—

But matched the shadow.

Then the shadow-Kaelen leaned out of the water, smirking.

"...you were never just human..."

Kaelen stepped back, breath trembling.

"What are you trying to show me?"

The shadow's reflection crawled out of the water.

"...you chase answers...

...but you fear the question..."

Kaelen shouted:

"SHOW YOURSELF!"

The reflection shattered into unbreath.

III. The Unheard Reveals the Devastating Truth

The Unheard approached Kaelen slowly, as if afraid the truth might break him more than the memories.

"Kaelen," he whispered.

"I have something to tell you. Something your mother never wanted you to know."

Kaelen stiffened.

"My mother...?"

The Unheard nodded.

"She came to the Thinker's Abyss before you were born. You knew that much."

"Yes," Kaelen whispered. "You told me she carried something back."

The Unheard closed his eyes.

"She did more than that."

Kaelen felt wind tighten around him.

"What are you saying?"

The Unheard looked directly into Kaelen's eyes.

"Your mother did not return from the abyss pregnant."

Kaelen's heart skipped.

"What—?"

"She returned with a breath.

Not a child.

A wind.

A fragment of the Primordials lost during the First Fracture."

Kaelen shook his head violently.

"No. I'm not—

I can't be—"

The Unheard placed a hand on his chest.

"Your soul, Kaelen...

is not human."

Kaelen staggered backward.

"But I had a body... I grew up... I—"

"Yes," the Unheard said softly. "Because your mother gave you one."

Kaelen froze.

"Explain."

The Unheard breathed in.

"Your mother carried an empty vessel inside her. A stillborn child. A life without breath."

Kaelen felt his knees weaken.

"She walked into the abyss with a child who could not live. She walked out with you."

Silence.

Heavy, impossible silence.

Kaelen whispered:

"I... replaced him?"

"No," the Unheard said.

"He and you became one.

Your body is human.

Your breath is not."

Kaelen clutched his head.

"Then what am I?"

The Unheard answered:

"You are a wind wearing flesh."

IV. The Seventh Wind Evolves — The Breath Beyond Identity

Kaelen fell to his knees.

He couldn't breathe.

He couldn't think.

He couldn't exist.

His breaths became shards.

His memories flickered.

His identity warped.

He screamed—

but no sound emerged.

Wind tore open around him.
Fragment.
Silence.
Heat.
Frost.
Storm.
Unbreath.
All spiraled violently.
The Unheard tried to reach him—
but couldn't approach.
Kaelen's wind was breaking him.
Kaelen gasped:
"I'm not real—
I'm not human—
I'm—"
The shadow's whisper echoed:
"...identity is fragile...
...allow me to break it..."
Kaelen snapped.
His body dissolved into swirling wind — a raw, primal form of
breath.
The Seventh Wind had begun its next evolution:
The Breath Beyond Identity.
Not a wind tied to a body.
Not a breath tied to a past.
A wind that could exist without form.
The Unheard watched in awe.
"Kaelen...
you're becoming something only the Primordials ever were."
Kaelen's wind-form stabilized.
His voice echoed without a mouth:
"I am not human."
Wind pulsed.

"I am not shadow."

Air rippled.

"I am not prophecy."

Silence hummed.

"I am the breath between truths."

The corridor trembled.

The Seventh Wind had evolved.

V. The Chapter Ends with a Trap

A cold voice echoed:

"...then you are ready..."

Kaelen turned—

And saw his shadow standing at the end of the corridor.

Not wearing a stolen face.

Wearing his true face.

The face Kaelen had before his mother retrieved him from the abyss.

A Kaelen that never lived.

A Kaelen who should have been born.

A Kaelen who died before breath touched him.

His shadow smirked:

"...you hunt me...

...but I am what you were meant to be..."

Kaelen whispered:

"You... are the child that died."

The shadow stepped forward.

"No. I am the breath that was denied.

And I am taking back what should have been mine."

Kaelen charged.

The shadow vanished.

And the chapter ends with:

Kaelen standing alone in the memory corridor, facing his own unborn self.

1 ¹ "THE NAMELESS CHAMBER"
Location: The Depth of the Memory Corridor
Identity's Origin

Kaelen followed his shadow deeper into the shifting corridor of stolen lives, the place where memories flickered like dying embers. His body had become partly wind, partly flesh, partly something new — a presence able to exist in spaces where no normal breath could survive.

The Unheard drifted behind him, tense.

"You feel it, don't you?" Kaelen whispered.

"Yes," the Unheard replied. "We're leaving the memory corridor. We're entering the birthplace of identity. The place where names are chosen... or erased."

A door appeared ahead.

No stone.

No wood.

No metal.

A door made of pure wind—shimmering, shifting, unanchored. Runes formed and dissolved across its surface: names unborn, names forgotten, names stolen.

Kaelen reached out.

The door inhaled.

It inhaled him.

Wind swallowed him whole.

I. The Chamber with No Name

Kaelen fell into a room of impossible dimensions — wide yet narrow, tall yet crushingly close. The walls were made of wind that carried whispers of every name ever spoken... and names that had never belonged to anyone.

Names floated like dust motes.

Some glowed.

Some trembled.

Some cried.

Some begged.

Some faded.

The Unheard bowed his head.

"This is the Nameless Chamber," he whispered.

"The place where identity is forged from breath."

Kaelen shivered.

"What was I before I had a name?"

The Unheard hesitated — then pointed.

At the far end of the chamber stood Kaelen's shadow.

Only now it was not wearing Kaelen's face.

It was wearing the face of the unborn child Kaelen had fused with — the life that never lived.

The shadow extended its arms.

Around it, names began to rot.

"...welcome home..."

II. The Shadow Prepares the Ritual

The shadow stepped into the center of the chamber, where a swirling vortex of wind formed a ritual circle.

Kaelen recognized it instantly.

"The Erasure Ritual."

The Unheard whispered:

"No. Worse.

This is the Overwriting Ritual — where one identity replaces another completely."

Kaelen's chest tightened.

The shadow smiled.

"...you stole my body, Kaelen...

my breath...

my mother...
my fate..."
Kaelen took a step back.
"No. I became what you could not. We share—"
"...NOTHING!"
The chamber shook.
Names exploded into dust.
Wind screamed.
Identity bled.
The shadow raised its hands.
Identity threads ripped from the walls and spiraled into the ritual circle — stolen Sirocco names, Zephyr names, Tempest titles, Wisper monikers, Mistral ancestries.
The shadow whispered:
"...I will overwrite you...
and become the Seventh Wind."
Kaelen roared:
"I won't let you take what I've become!"
The shadow smiled.
"...I'm not taking what you became.
I'm taking what you ARE."
The ritual ignited.

III. Kaelen Is Pulled into the Ritual

The chamber tightened around Kaelen like a coffin of wind.
He gasped as the ritual threads latched onto him:
One pulled at his childhood
Another pulled at his breath
Another pulled at his memories
Another pulled at his future
Another pulled at his identity
The shadow spoke:
"...you are a breath wearing flesh...
I am the flesh denied its breath..."

Kaelen felt identity stripping away.

He screamed.

The Unheard tried to intervene — but the chamber denied him entry.

"No!" Kaelen cried.
"Don't you touch him!"

The shadow leaned close.

"...you should never have existed..."

Kaelen's voice broke.

"Then I will fight for my right to live."

The ritual reached its peak—

And Kaelen vanished into blinding wind.

12 "BREATHLESS WAR"

Location: Whispered Plateau (Real World)

While Kaelen was trapped in the Chamber, the clans spiraled into full-scale war.

No leadership.

No trust.

No truth.

No breath that could be believed.

Sirocco blamed Mistral for the identity theft.

Mistral blamed Zephyr for memory manipulation.

Zephyr blamed Wisper for silence that masked deception.

Tempest blamed everyone.

Wisper blamed the very concept of identity.

Battles erupted across the plateau.

Heatstorms collided with frost-ridges.

Lightning shattered flicker-paths.

Silence strangled storm roars.

Fragments sliced through breath.

Unbreath consumed memories mid-fight.

It was chaos given form.

The Scorched Sovereign shouted over the melee:

"This isn't war — THIS IS SUICIDE!"

But the clans were deaf to reason.

Identity had become meaningless.

Trust had become poison.

Breath had become weapon.

They would tear the world apart.

Unless Kaelen returned.

I. The Shadow Attacks the Battlefield Directly

Then the worst happened.

The death-wind Kaelen stepped onto the plateau...

wearing the face of the Tempestborn.

He raised his hands.

Wind folded.

And entire phalanxes disappeared without a sound.

Sirocco warriors screamed.

Zephyr flickers failed to dodge.

Mistral frost shattered.

Tempest lightning broke against nothing.

Wisper shadows fled their own silhouettes.

The shadow whispered through stolen breaths:

"...I am the wind that ends identity..."

The clans screamed:

"THE TEMPESTBORN HAS BETRAYED US!"

More war.

More death.

More erasure.

The Unheard appeared amid the chaos.

He whispered desperately:

"Kaelen... hurry... we are dying..."

13

"THE WIND THAT REMEMBERS"

Location: Nameless Chamber
Birthplace of the Seventh Wind

K aelen hung suspended between winds.
His identity unraveling.
His memories splitting.
His destiny bleeding.
The shadow approached him.
"...goodbye, Kaelen..."
Kaelen whispered:
"...no..."
The shadow blinked.
"...what?"
Kaelen inhaled.
Deep.
Deeper than he ever had before.
He inhaled the memories cracking around him.
He inhaled the history of the wind.
He inhaled the forgotten names.
He inhaled the Primordial whispers.
He inhaled himself.
Then he spoke:
"I am not just a wind wearing flesh.
I am a memory wearing destiny.
And I... remember."
The Nameless Chamber shuddered.
Wind began to gather behind Kaelen.
Not seven winds.
Something older.

Something deeper.

Something the Primordials had hinted at.

A wind that remembers.

The shadow screamed:

"NO — THAT WIND SHOULD NOT EXIST!"

Kaelen opened his eyes.

They glowed with a new breath:

The Remembered Wind — the lost counterpart to the Unbreath.

The wind that holds identity together.

Kaelen whispered:

"You are the breath that destroys identity.

I am the breath that restores it."

The shadow lunged.

Kaelen exhaled—

And identity flooded the chamber.

Memories returned.

Names reformed.

Stolen selves were restored.

The ritual shattered.

The shadow was thrown violently backward.

"No... NO... this is impossible!"

Kaelen drifted forward, wind swirling like luminous threads.

"It's time you learned something, shadow."

He placed his hand on his double's chest.

"I am the Seventh Wind because I am the wind that remembers."

The shadow howled:

"IF YOU REMEMBER,

I CANNOT STEAL!"

Kaelen whispered:

"And if you cannot steal...

you cannot exist."

He exhaled a final pulse.

The shadow cracked—

fractured—

shattered into unbreath—

and fled screaming into the void.

Kaelen collapsed, exhausted but alive.

The Unheard knelt beside him.

"Kaelen... what did you do?"

Kaelen, barely conscious, whispered:

"I reconnected myself."

He stood — barely — as the chamber dissolved around him.

And with the Seventh Wind restored...

He returned to the battlefield.

K aelen emerges reborn, carrying:
    The Remembered Wind (his next evolution)
The knowledge of his birth
The ability to fight identity theft directly
A new destiny that terrifies the shadow and the clans alike
Meanwhile:
The shadow has retreated to rebuild
The clans are in catastrophic war
The world is tearing itself apart

Part III

1 "RETURN OF THE SEVENTH WIND"
Location: Whispered Plateau
Present Time

Wind tore across the battlefield.

Heatstorms burned trenches into the stone.

Frostborne ridges split the air with jagged force.

Lightning spiraled downward in shattered arcs.

Silence cut through breath like a blade.

Fragments flickered in violent loops.

Unbreath devoured the shadows of fallen warriors.

The clans — already exhausted from fear, betrayal, and mimicry — were killing each other blindly.

Everywhere, shouts rose:

"He's an impostor—!"

"Her shadow moved—!"

"That's not my captain—!"

"IDENTITY IS BROKEN!"

In the dead center of the chaos stood the Tempestborn, barely conscious, trying to rally his fractured army.

The Scorched Sovereign fought two Sirocco elites who believed she had been overwritten.

The Fragmented Master flickered uncontrollably, unable to stabilize.

Black Wisper assassins formed a trembling perimeter, paralyzed by too many false shadows.

The world trembled on the edge of collapse.

Then—

Wind stopped.

Not slowed.
Not silenced.
Stopped.
All breath held as if the world itself inhaled...
...and forgot to exhale.
A pulse crossed the battlefield — soft, luminous, impossible.
And Kaelen stepped into the plateau.

I. The Return of the Seventh Wind

He wasn't walking.
He was descending on wind that remembered him.
Not storm.
Not silence.
Not flame.
Not frost.
Not fragment.
Not unbreath.
A new breath.
A breath of memory.
The Remembered Wind spiraled around his body like threads of ancient light. His eyes glowed with shifting names — identities he had restored. His voice echoed with the steady hum of truth.
He stepped forward.
Each footfall realigned the battlefield.
Frost melted.
Heat cooled.
Lightning bent away.
Silence softened.
Fragments straightened.
Unbreath recoiled.
Warriors who still had their identities gasped.
Warriors who had lost theirs began to feel memories again.
Names.

Faces.

Purposes.

The Seventh Wind had returned — and he brought himself back with him.

II. Every Clan Reacts

Sirocco

Heat-born leaders knelt as memory returned to warriors who had forgotten their ranks.

Mistral

Frost masks cracked as ancient lineage names pulsed in their minds again.

Zephyr

Broken flickers stabilized; they could see their true movements.

Tempest

Lightning softened around the Tempestborn; he whispered Kaelen's name with something between shame and relief.

Black Wisper

Silence bowed to him.

Not as a master.

As recognition.

Kaelen breathed in every reaction.

The battlefield steadied.

But not for long.

Because the world felt the shift.

III. Foreshadowing the Next Novels — Three Omens Appear

As Kaelen stepped deeper into the plateau, the wind thickened, heavy with unseen truths.

Three omens emerged — each tied to a future book.

OMEN I — *The Eighth Pulse*

A faint vibration only Kaelen feels

A ripple crossed the sky — soft, nearly unnoticed, but Kaelen felt it vibrate through his bones.

He whispered:

"...that wasn't any of the Seven Winds."

The Unheard stiffened.

"Kaelen... what did you feel?"

He hesitated.

"A wind with no memory.
A breath with no origin.
An Eighth Wind."

OMEN II — *The Windless Horizon*
The sky flickers as if something is draining breath itself

Far on the horizon, the sky dimmed — not by cloud, shadow, or storm.

It dimmed because something was removing wind itself.

Kaelen inhaled and felt...

Nothing.

A piece of the world had no breath.

A Windless Zone.

"Impossible..." the Scorched Sovereign whispered. "That region is... dying?"

Kaelen's stomach turned.

"No.

Something is stealing wind."

OMEN III — *The Shadow's Master*
Kaelen hears a whisper that is not the shadow
The death-wind Kaelen had fled into the void...
But now Kaelen heard a new voice inside the wind:
"...you remember now...
...but do you know what you truly are?"
Not the shadow.
Not the Unbreath.
Someone deeper.
Someone older.
A will behind the shadow.
Kaelen whispered:
"That voice...
I've heard it before..."
The Unheard froze.
"You are not ready for that name."

IV. Kaelen Calls for Peace — The Winds Answer

Kaelen raised both hands.

Wind swirled behind him — a sweeping arc of unity.

His voice carried across the plateau:

"ENOUGH!"

The winds obeyed.

Heat bent to stillness.

Frost melted into mist.

Lightning settled into the ground.

Silence thickened but did not cut.

Fragments aligned.

Unbreath retreated.

Sirocco stopped fighting.

Zephyr flickers stabilized.

Mistral lowered their weapons.

Tempest froze mid-strike.

Wisper shadows softened.

Kaelen continued:

"You fight mirrors.

You fight memories.

You fight fears."

Wind pulsed brighter.

"But the true enemy is coming —

and it will not care who you are."

The clans stared.

Kaelen exhaled.

Every warrior felt their identity pulse inside them with new clarity.

He whispered:

"Unite now...

or watch the world lose breath."

V. The Death-Wind Kaelen Returns

Wind twisted like a corrupted reflection.

A familiar figure stepped out of a tear in the sky.

Not fully formed.

Not fully shadow.

A fractured Kaelen-shape trembling with unstable identities.

The death-wind Kaelen hissed:

"...you remember yourself...

...but can you remember how to kill me?"

Kaelen stepped forward.

"No.

I won't kill you."

The shadow tilted its head mockingly.

"...mercy?"

"No," Kaelen said, eyes glowing with Remembered Wind.

"Because you're not my final enemy."

The shadow's smile dropped.

Behind it...

something bigger stirred.

Something older.

Something that did not belong to any known wind.

A pulse shook the plateau.

The clans gasped.

Kaelen whispered:

"...the Eighth Wind..."

And the chapter ends with the sky cracking—

just once—

as something vast, hollow, and ancient begins to awaken.

2   "THE ECHO OF THE EIGHTH WIND"
Location: Whispered Plateau
Between War and Awakening

Wind trembled.
Not from storm.
Not from silence.
Not from heat.
Not from frost.
Not from broken-motion.
Not from unbreath.
Not even from Kaelen's Remembered Wind.
Something older.
Something quieter.
Something wrong.
A pulse rippled across the sky, faint as a dying whisper but felt in the bones of every warrior.
The air twitched.
The plateau stilled.
Kaelen took one slow, uneasy inhale.
"...that wasn't any of ours."
The Unheard floated beside him, his form dimming.
"I felt no breath in it."
"Then what was it?" Kaelen whispered.
The Unheard's voice cracked for the first time in the series:
"An echo of... nothing."

I. The Eighth Wind Reveals a Fragment of Its Nature

The horizon shimmered — not with heat, not with storm, not with shadow.

It shimmered with absence.

A patch of sky flickered like a broken memory.

A low vibration spread through the ground, rattling stone and bone alike.

Warriors clutched their chests.

Flicker-walkers stumbled.

Wisper assassins gasped — startled by feeling anything involuntarily.

Kaelen gripped his chest.

His breath... stuttered.

Every wind inside him recoiled.

Frost.

Flame.

Storm.

Fragment.

Silence.

Unbreath.

Even the Remembered Wind —

—all shrank as if recoiling from a predator.

Kaelen whispered, terrified:

"That's not wind...

it's anti-breath."

The Unheard nodded.
"The Eighth Wind...
is the breath that was never born."

I**I. The Clans Experience the First Symptoms**

Sirocco

Heat evaporated from their breath. Flames sputtered out.
Their wind felt suddenly cold.
A warrior screamed:
"My wind... died."

Mistral

Frost cracked violently across their armor as if their lineage memories were snapping.
They felt a heavy grief rise — the loss of ancestral breath.

Zephyr

Flicker-steps malfunctioned.
Movements froze mid-stride.
Time itself stuttered around them.
"We can't enter motion... motion is missing."

Tempest

Lightning formed but refused to discharge — stuck, caught, strangled.
The Tempestborn fell to one knee, trembling.
"Storm... can't breathe..."

Black Wisper

Silence grew too deep.
Voices couldn't form.
Even thoughts became muffled.
A Wisper elder whispered through bleeding shadows:
"This is not our silence."

*K*aelen
Every breath he carried—
the balanced, unified, stabilizing Seventh Wind—
BEGIN TO UNRAVEL.
He gasped, clutching his chest.
"It's erasing the concept of wind—"
The Unheard caught him before he fell.
"No.
It is erasing the origin of wind.
The very idea that breath creates identity."
Kaelen's eyes widened.
"Then it's hunting the Primordials."
The Unheard whispered:
"It may be older than them."

II. The Death-Wind Kaelen Panics

The shadow, standing across the plateau, suddenly convulsed.

Its form flickered through ALL stolen identities at once:

Sirocco → Mistral → Zephyr → Tempest → Wisper → Kaelen → the unborn child → a nameless silhouette → a blank, featureless void.

It screamed in a voice not meant for a throat:

"NO! NOT THAT ONE!"

Kaelen froze.

He had never seen his shadow afraid.

The shadow's voice trembled:

"YOU FOOL—THE EIGHTH WIND DOES NOT MIMIC. IT DEVOURS IDENTITY ENTIRELY!"

Kaelen took a step forward.

"You know what it is?"

The shadow snarled:

"IT IS WHY THE PRIMORDIALS FRACTURED! IT IS WHY THE SIX WINDS SPLIT! IT IS WHY THE SEVENTH WAS LOST!"

Kaelen's heart pounded.

"What does it want?"

The shadow looked directly at him — terrified.

"...to finish the job."

IV. A Vision — The Eighth Wind's Domain

The world blinked.

Kaelen suddenly stood in a place with no sound, no time, no breath.

A void.

A flat horizon of pale white nothing.

In the distance, something moved.

Not shape.

Not wind.

Not shadow.

A cancellation.

Where it passed, reality melted like frost under flame.

Kaelen tried to breathe—

And nothing entered his lungs.

His body began to distort.

His memories flickered.

His name... flickered.

He reached for the Remembered Wind—

it collapsed.

He reached for the Seventh—

it dimmed.

He reached for ANY wind—

nothing answered.

A whisper crawled across the void:

"...return to stillness..."

Kaelen fell to his knees.

"Stop... STOP—"

"...return to the age before breath..."

Kaelen's vision dimmed.

His identity... failed.

Then—

A burst of golden-blue wind pulled him violently back into reality.

The Unheard stood over him, glowing with desperate silence.

"You cannot touch it," the Unheard gasped.

"Not yet."

V. Kaelen's New Fear — His Wind Can Die

Kaelen got to his feet trembling.

"What... was that place?"

The Unheard looked shaken.

"That was the Eighth Wind's domain:

The Hollow Horizon.

Where wind goes to die."

Kaelen's breath shook.

"I felt myself fading.

My name fading."

"That is its purpose," the Unheard whispered.

"It is the anti-wind.

The wind that erases breath, identity, memory... existence."

Kaelen clenched his fists.

"Can it be fought?"

The Unheard hesitated.

"...Kaelen...

I do not know if it can even be understood."

VI. Kaelen Makes a Vow

Kaelen stood at the center of the battlefield, wind swirling uneasily around him.

He whispered:

"I am the Seventh Wind...
the wind that remembers."
He inhaled—
and every identity on the plateau shimmered with clarity.
"But memory alone is not enough."
He looked at the trembling horizon, where the Eighth Wind pulsed again.
"I must become more than wind."
Lightning cracked overhead.
Shadows twisted.
Heat flickered.
Frost whispered.
Silence bowed.
Even the death-wind stared.
Kaelen raised his hand.
"For this world to live...
I must remember EVERYTHING the winds have forgotten."
The sky trembled.

3 "THE HOLLOW HORIZON"
Location: Outer Edge of the Whispered Plateau
Boundary of the Hollow Horizon

The battlefield lay quiet for the first time in days.

Not peaceful.

Not resolved.

Quiet in the way a wounded animal is quiet.

The winds trembled uneasily across the scarred landscape as Kaelen approached the edge of the world's newest wound — the Hollow Horizon, where the Eighth Wind had first pulsed.

The air near it was wrong.

Wind did not move.

Sound did not travel.

Shadows did not align.

Light bent inward, like the world was being swallowed by its own reflection.

Kaelen inhaled.

The Remembered Wind inside him flickered nervously.

He whispered:

"This place... shouldn't exist."

The Unheard hovered beside him, his own form dim with strain.

"It didn't," he replied. "Until something called it."

Kaelen nodded.

He already suspected who.

Behind him, the clans stood at a distance, unsure whether they were watching their salvation or their executioner.

Sirocco heat died near the horizon.

Mistral frost evaporated into nothing.

Zephyr steps faltered.

Tempest lightning grounded itself.

Wisper silence dissolved.

Even the death-wind Kaelen — standing in the distance — refused to step closer.

Kaelen took another breath.

The world held its own.

I. Kaelen Tests the Boundary

He kneeled and placed his hands on the ground.

Wind gathered in a familiar swirl behind him:

Concordia

Resonantia

Equalis

Remembered Breath

The Seventh Wind

All five harmonized.

He focused them toward the pale, trembling edge of the Hollow Horizon.

The moment they touched it—

The winds died.

Not broke.

Not scattered.

Not resisted.

Died.

Kaelen recoiled as if burned.

"What—"

The Unheard finished the sentence, trembling:

"Nothing can exist inside the Eighth Wind's domain."

Kaelen inhaled slowly.

"I'm going in."

The Unheard grabbed his shoulder.

"Kaelen. Listen to me."

Kaelen met his gaze.

"You won't come back."

Kaelen nodded once.

"I know."

Wind tightened around him.

Sirocco's Scorched Sovereign called out:

"Seventh Wind! If you enter, you may lose your breath!"

Mistral's envoy shouted:

"You may lose your memories!"

Zephyr flickers cried:

"You may lose your identity!"

Tempestborn whispered:

"You may lose yourself."

Kaelen closed his eyes.

"That's the risk."

He stepped forward.

The world dimmed around him.

Then—

Kaelen entered the Hollow Horizon.

II. Inside the Hollow

Wind vanished.

Color vanished.

Sound vanished.

Time hesitated, unsure if it should move.

Kaelen walked through an endless flat plain made of pale, shifting non-light. His body felt lighter than silence but heavier than stone.

The Remembered Wind inside him trembled violently, trying to retreat.

Kaelen whispered:

"It's okay. Stay with me."

But a voice rose.

Not the Eighth Wind.

His shadow.

"...you shouldn't be here..."
Kaelen turned.
But instead of a single shadow, he saw—
A thousand Kaelens.
Each one a different version of him:
The Kaelen who never entered the abyss
The Kaelen the death-wind wanted to overwrite
The Kaelen the Primordials imagined
The Kaelen his mother might have had
The Kaelen he feared becoming
The Kaelen who died in infancy
All standing in an endless field of ghosts.
All staring at him.
Kaelen stumbled backward.
"No... you're not real—"
Every version spoke together:
"...not real?
Or too real?"
Kaelen gasped.
He heard identity... unraveling.

III. The Eighth Wind Makes Contact

Windless silence split open.
A shape appeared in the distance.
A ripple.
A distortion.
A tear.
Not a being.
Not a memory.
A cancellation of existence walking on nothing.
Kaelen tried to breathe—
And nothing entered.
His lungs seized.

His name flickered.

His purpose dimmed.

His memories blurred.

The Eighth Wind spoke with a voice of erased futures:

"...return to the age before breath..."

Kaelen coughed, choking on non-air.

"I... I... remember—"

"...memory is a wound..."

"I—am—the—Seventh—Wind—"

"...wind is an illusion..."

Kaelen collapsed to one knee.

Identity... slipping.

He whispered hoarsely:

"Stop... STOP—"

But the Eighth Wind whispered back:

"...I do not stop.

I unmake."

IV. Kaelen's First Adaptation — The Remembered Wind Defies Erasure

Kaelen felt himself dissolving.

His breath disappearing.

His thoughts fragmenting.

His identity fading into pale light.

But then—

A spark ignited inside him.

A memory.

His mother's face.

Her voice saying his name for the first time.

"Kaelen."

The Remembered Wind pulsed with the force of a hundred forgotten lifetimes.

Kaelen inhaled—

And breath surged into him from a place older than wind.

He rose, barely standing.

"Identity... is not an illusion."

The Eighth Wind paused.

Kaelen took another trembling breath.

"It is memory.

It is choice.

It is breath given shape.

And I am the wind that remembers."

The Eighth Wind shuddered.

It spoke again:

"...you are unstable... unfinished... incomplete..."

Kaelen exhaled slowly.

"I'm evolving."

The Remembered Wind wrapped around him like a protective cocoon.

For the first time, the Eighth Wind stepped back.

And Kaelen stepped forward.

One breath deeper into the Hollow.

V. Kaelen Escapes the Horizon — Barely

The Eighth Wind pulsed again.

Kaelen felt identity leaking from him.

He stumbled backward, the Remembered Wind vibrating violently.

The Unheard's voice echoed faintly:

"KAELEN—COME BACK!"

Kaelen reached out—

And the Remembered Wind exploded around him, pushing him violently out of the Hollow Horizon.

He crashed onto the Whispered Plateau.

Warriors screamed and stepped back.

The Unheard caught him.

"You... survived..."

Kaelen could barely speak.

"I found it."

"Found what?" the Unheard asked.

Kaelen looked up at the trembling horizon.

"The Eighth Wind," he whispered, "is not trying to kill us."

The clans froze.

Then what?"

Kaelen stood, steadying himself.

"It's trying to return the world to what existed before wind."

The clans gasped.

The Unheard whispered:

"...the end of breath."

Kaelen nodded.

"And now... it knows I can enter its domain."

Wind shivered across the plateau.

The war was no longer about identity.

It was about existence.

4 "THE ARCHITECT'S WHISPER"
Location: Whispered Plateau
Edge of the Hollow Horizon
Inside Kaelen's mind

Wind trembled around Kaelen like a fearful animal.
Not from cold.
Not from heat.
Not from storm.
Not from shadow.

Because the wind had heard something before Kaelen did —
and it recoiled.

The Remembered Wind inside him flickered violently, as if
trying to hide.

Kaelen stood on the edge of the Hollow Horizon again, staring into the pale distortion where the Eighth Wind pulsed.

He whispered:

"I know you're watching."

Wind twisted.

Silence deepened.

The Unheard, hovering behind him, stiffened.

"You feel it too?" Kaelen asked.

The Unheard didn't answer.

He couldn't.

His shadows trembled uncontrollably.

Kaelen frowned.

"What's wrong?"

The Unheard whispered, voice breaking:

"I hear... no silence."

Kaelen froze.

Silence was the Wisper's domain.
For him to hear no silence meant one thing:
Something older
something deeper
something absolute
had entered their reality.
Then—
A voice spoke.
Not from the horizon.
Not from the wind.
Not from the Unheard.
Not from the shadow.
It spoke from within Kaelen's breath.

I. The First Whisper

A faint vibration rolled through his lungs.
Not painful.
Not forceful.
Inevitable.
Kaelen inhaled sharply.
"What—"
The voice whispered again:
"...still you breathe..."
Kaelen stumbled backward, clutching his throat.
"Who—who are you?"
The whisper curled around his breath like a cold hand:
"...little wind...
you wear a name that was never meant for you..."
Kaelen's heart slammed in his chest.
The Unheard rushed forward, shadows shaking violently.
"Kaelen—run—NOW—"
Kaelen's body locked in place.
"I... can't..."
The voice pulsed again:

"...do not command him, echo...
he belongs to me..."
The Unheard recoiled as if struck.
"NO," the Unheard gasped, shadows collapsing.
"NO ONE commands wind—NOT EVEN YOU—"
The whisper deepened.
"...I am not wind..."
Kaelen's breath faltered.
The Unheard screamed:
"KAELEN, SHUT YOUR MIND—"
Too late.
The voice filled Kaelen's thoughts with a cold, impossible truth:
"...I am the breathless architect...
and you are the flaw I intend to correct..."
Kaelen's vision blurred.
"I'm... a flaw?"
The whisper caressed the inside of his skull:
"...you were never supposed to exist...
you are the memory that escaped my design..."
Kaelen gasped, collapsing to his knees.
He felt something ancient and intelligent crawl through his thoughts, dissecting him, analyzing him, searching him.
The voice chuckled softly — a sound without sound.
"...tell me, Seventh Wind...
do you know why your mother went into the abyss?"
Kaelen's blood turned to ice.
"She—she was looking for—"
"...a child she could not have..."
Kaelen froze.
The whisper pressed deeper.
"...so she reached into my domain...
and stole the breath I cast away..."

Kaelen's heart cracked.

"She... stole me?"

"...you are an error...
a breath I discarded...
a memory I rejected..."

Kaelen felt himself unraveling.

Identity... slipping.
Purpose... wavering.
Breath... collapsing.

The Unheard launched himself between Kaelen and the horizon, shouting:

"ENOUGH!"

Shadows erupted from him, forming a cocoon around Kaelen.

"YOU DO NOT TOUCH HIM!"

But the whisper simply passed through.

"...you have no authority here, echo..."

The Unheard screamed as his shadow cracked.

Kaelen crawled forward, breath shaking.

"Why... are you doing this...?"

The whisper answered:

"...to return the world to stillness...
to silence the age of wind...
to erase the memory of breath..."

Kaelen's eyes widened.

"You want... the end of the winds."

"...I designed the world to be still...
it is you winds who defy the original shape..."

Kaelen clenched his fists.

"I won't let you."

A soft, amused exhale rippled through the horizon.

"...you cannot stop what existed before breath..."

T hen the whisper sharpened:
    "...Seventh Wind...
I will unmake you last...
so you may remember the end."
    The voice faded like a nightmare slipping away—
    but the terror did not.
    The Unheard fell to his knees, shadows leaking from his
form.
    Kaelen stared at the horizon, trembling.
    "What... what was that?"
    The Unheard gasped one answer:
    "The Architect of Unbreath."
    Kaelen looked at his hands.
    They were shaking uncontrollably.
    Not from fear—
    from truth.
    Because the Architect's whisper had left one final imprint in-
side him:
    A vision.
    A possible future.
    He saw himself—
    standing alone
in a world with no wind
no breath
no identity
no life

holding the last memory of existence.
The Seventh Wind...
as the only breath left in a hollow world.

5 "THE LAST BREATH CONCLAVE"
Location: The Shattered Amphitheater

A sacred meeting ground abandoned since the First Storm War

The ancient amphitheater rose from the broken plateau like a scar: a ring of stone carved with wind-runes so old even the clans had forgotten who carved them.

But tonight, for the first time in centuries, all five clans gathered inside it.

Sirocco's banners smoldered with restrained heat.
Mistral's frost veiled their ranks in thin white mist.
Tempest's storm-capes crackled with unsettled lightning.
Zephyr's flicker-walkers stood in fractured formation.
Black Wisper's silhouettes hovered at the edges, forming a perimeter of quiet dread.

And in the center—
Kaelen stood alone.
The Seventh Wind.
The wind they feared.
The wind they needed.
The wind they did not yet trust.

The Unheard hovered at his back, weakened but resolute.
Kaelen exhaled slowly.
The Remembered Wind pulsed once, steady and bright.
Then Kaelen spoke.

I. The Conclave Begins

"Clans of Wind," Kaelen said, voice ringing with the harmony of a hundred forgotten breaths.

"We stand on the edge of a horizon that should never exist."

Mistral's envoy stepped forward.

"What did you see inside that abyss?"

Zephyr's commander flickered beside him.

"What hunts us?"

Sirocco's Scorched Sovereign folded her arms.

"And why should we believe you?"

Kaelen nodded.

He expected the hostility.

He welcomed it.

"Because I am the only one who survived the Hollow Horizon," he said.

"And the only one who has heard the voice of the thing waiting inside it."

Tempestborn stepped forward, jaw clenched.

A crackle of unspent thunder ran down his arm.

"You said its name before you collapsed," he said quietly.

"The Architect of Unbreath."

Mistral warriors whispered nervously.

Sirocco spat the name like poison.

Zephyr flickered in and out of sight.

Black Wisper's shapes deepened with unease.

Kaelen raised a hand.

"That is why we are here."

II. Kaelen Reveals the Unthinkable Truth

Kaelen breathed deeply.

Wind stilled.

Silence tightened.

Heat lowered.

Frost grew still.

Storm grounded.

Fragment steadied.

Every breath on the plateau listened.

"The Architect of Unbreath is older than the Primordial Winds," Kaelen said.

"Older than the First Breath.

Older than identity."

Tempestborn paled.

Sirocco's sovereign scoffed—but too sharply, too nervously.

Mistral shivered, frost trembling on their armor.

Kaelen continued:

"It created the Eighth Wind—the Hollow Wind.

The wind that doesn't give breath...

but erases it."

The amphitheater erupted with panic.

"How can a wind erase wind?!"

"That breaks every law of breath!"

"Impossible—unless the world was built to fail!"

"Does Kaelen speak truth, or prophecy?!"

"Or madness?"

Kaelen raised his hand, and the Seventh Wind resonated.

Sound dimmed.

The Conclave fell silent.

"The Architect's goal is simple," Kaelen said softly.

"To erase every wind.

To erase identity.

To erase breath.

To return the world to the stillness it was meant to be."

Zephyr's commander stepped back, flickering in fear.

"You mean... the end of existence?"

Kaelen nodded.

"The end of breath."

III. The Clans Demand Answers

Sirocco's leader pointed a burning finger at him.

"Why tell us now?"

Mistral's envoy added:

"Why entrust this truth to clans who nearly killed each other?"

Tempestborn clenched his fists.

"Why would the Architect unmake the winds it once created?"

Kaelen answered the last question first.

"It never created the winds.

It created a world without them."

The Unheard stepped forward, shadows trembling.

"And when the Primordial Winds arose—born of defiance, choice, identity—

they ruined the Architect's perfect stillness."

Zephyr's ranks gasped.

Mistral whispered prayers.

Sirocco cursed violently.

Tempestborn staggered.

Kaelen swallowed hard.

"And now it wants to finish what it started."

IV. The Shadow Kaelen Interrupts the Conclave

A flicker of darkness tore across the amphitheater.

Not a wind.

Not a breath.

A wound.

Kaelen turned sharply.

His shadow stepped into the center, wearing a fractured version of his face.

Half-identity.

Half-void.

Half-memory.

Half-unbreath.

Warriors reached for weapons.

Kaelen did not.

The shadow bowed mockingly.

"You gathered them well, Seventh Wind."

Sirocco flames surged.

Mistral frost cracked.

Zephyr flickers vanished.

Wisper shadows sharpened.

Tempest lightning rose.

Kaelen raised a hand.

"Let him speak."

The clans recoiled.

The shadow grinned.

"You reveal the Architect's intent. How noble."

Kaelen's jaw tightened.

"Why come here, shadow?"

"To warn you."

Silence thickened.

Even the Unheard flinched.

The shadow continued:

"You tell them what the Architect wants. But not what it plans. Not what it will take."

Tempestborn stepped forward.

"And what will it take?"

The shadow lowered its voice to a chilling whisper.

"A sacrifice."

Kaelen's stomach dropped.

"What kind of sacrifice?"

The shadow looked directly into Kaelen's eyes.

"Yours."

V. The Clans Revolt Against Fate

Chaos erupted.

"He must be destroyed!"

"He's the Architect's weakness!"

"No—he's our only hope!"

"He may be the key OR the doorway!"

"The Seventh Wind cannot be trusted—!"

Mistral warriors looked horrified.

Sirocco warriors demanded Kaelen's execution.

Zephyr began to flicker away.

Tempestborn raised lightning.

Wisper shadows closed in.

But Kaelen did not flinch.

He stepped toward his shadow.

"Explain."

The shadow's smile faded.

"The Architect cannot erase the winds while you exist. You are the memory that shouldn't have survived. You are the breath that disobeyed."

Kaelen's heart hammered.

"So it wants to unmake me."

The shadow nodded.

"And if it succeeds...

the world will follow."

VI. Kaelen Makes His Stand

Kaelen turned back to the clans.

"Now do you understand?"

Silence.
Fear.
Realization.
Kaelen's voice grew stronger.
"We do not have the luxury of mistrust.
We do not have the luxury of civil war.
We do not have the luxury of pretending the Eighth Wind will spare anyone."
Wind pulsed around him, gentle but unyielding.
"If we do not unite now—
the world will become hollow."
Tempestborn stepped forward first.
He bowed his head.
"For the first time...
I follow another."
Sirocco's sovereign looked shaken, but nodded.
"Mistrust kept us alive.
Unity may keep us breathing."
Mistral's envoy lowered his frost.
"We will follow the Seventh Wind."
Zephyr flickered into alignment.
"We choose survival."
Black Wisper bowed in silence.
Kaelen inhaled.
He exhaled.
And the Conclave united.
But the shadow laughed.
"You have rallied them well, Seventh Wind.
Pity it won't matter."
Kaelen stepped forward.
"Why?"
The shadow pointed to the sky.
A crack spread across it.

A long, thin fracture—
the first tear of the Eighth Wind.

6 "TEAR IN THE SKY"
Location: The Shattered Amphitheater
The Open Plateau

The Conclave had barely united when the sky screamed.
A soundless scream—
felt, not heard.
A vibration in the bone.
A tremor in the breath.
A shudder in the identity.
Wind fled from the sound.
Kaelen looked up.
The sky was cracking.
A thin white line—
straight as a blade,
pale as bone,
cold as the Hollow Horizon—
split the heavens from horizon to horizon.
The first tear.
The death-wind Kaelen whispered:
"...it has begun..."
The Unheard trembled.
"That is not a fracture.
That is a threshold.
A doorway."
Kaelen swallowed hard.
"A doorway for what?"
The answer came in the form of silence so deep it erased the
wind itself.
The Eighth Wind.

I. The Tear Widens

The pale line pulsed once—
and every clan fell to their knees.
Zephyr flickers collapsed mid-step.
Sirocco flames died instantly.
Mistral frost sublimated into nothing.
Tempest lightning grounded in terror.
Wisper shadows curled inward like frightened children.
Even the shadow Kaelen staggered.
Kaelen remained standing—barely—as the Remembered Wind braced his lungs.
The sky pulsed again.
CRACK.
The pale line widened, splitting the heavens like torn cloth.
Through the gap, no stars shone.
No clouds drifted.
No light flickered.
Behind the tear was—
NOTHING.
A void of absolute stillness.
A preview of a world before breath.
Kaelen whispered:
"The Hollow Horizon... it's expanding into the sky."
The Unheard nodded shakily.
"This is how existence ends."

II. First Manifestation of the Eighth Wind

A shape moved behind the tear.

Not a body.

Not a storm.

Not a shadow.

A cancellation of form.

As it approached, the air bent inward like reality was being folded and smoothed out.

A whisper crawled across the amphitheater:

"...stillness returns..."

Kaelen felt his breath seize.

The Remembered Wind inside him writhed violently—
trying to hold his identity together.

The clans screamed as the Eighth Wind's presence approached.

Zephyr warriors dissolved into flicker-static.

Sirocco warriors clawed at their throats—no breath entering.

Mistral fell limp, frost erased.

Tempestborn roared in agony as lightning died inside him.

Black Wisper's silence collapsed into chaotic noise.

Kaelen forced himself forward.

"No... you can't... enter our world..."

The tear widened further—

and the Eighth Wind reached a limb-like distortion through the gap.

Not a hand.

Not a tendril.

A concept of erasure given shape.

The air bent around it.

The world bent around it.

Kaelen whispered:

"If it enters fully... nothing will survive."

III. Kaelen Confronts the Eighth Wind Directly

The Eighth Wind's limb brushed the amphitheater's edge—

Stone dissolved.
Wind vanished.
Identity went pale.

A Mistral warrior screamed as his own name burned off his breath—
and he collapsed into a blank, empty silhouette.

Kaelen ran toward the tear.

The Unheard shouted:

"KAELEN—NO! YOU CAN'T—"

But Kaelen didn't slow.

He activated the Remembered Wind—
the Seventh Wind surged behind him like a storm of luminous threads.

He leapt into the air—
and struck the limb of the Eighth Wind.

The world rippled.

The tear buckled.

Kaelen did not dissolve.

He was thrown back hundreds of feet—
slamming into stone—
but he lived.

Sirocco warriors gasped.

Zephyr stared.

Mistral bowed.

Tempestborn whispered:

"He... blocked it."

Kaelen rose shakily.

His voice trembled:

"I can't hurt it...
but I can slow it."

IV. The Eighth Wind Speaks Into Reality

The sky darkened.

The tear widened further.

And for the first time—
The Eighth Wind spoke directly into the physical world.
"...SEVENTH WIND..."
Every clan collapsed to their knees.
Every warrior clutched their head.
Kaelen alone remained standing—barely.
He shouted at the sky:
"THIS ISN'T YOUR WORLD!"
A soft exhale drifted through the tear.
Cold.
Unfeeling.
Absolute.
"...it was never yours..."
Kaelen's heart slammed in his chest.
"You will not return this world to stillness."
"...stillness is perfection..."
Kaelen roared:
"WIND IS LIFE!"
"...life is noise..."
Kaelen screamed:
"IDENTITY IS PURPOSE!"
The tear pulsed.
"...purpose is deviation..."
Kaelen staggered.
The Eighth Wind whispered:
"...you should not exist...
and neither should they..."
Kaelen clenched his fists.
"You're afraid of us."
The tear froze.
Then—
"...yes."
The world shook.

Kaelen jolted.

"What...?"

The Eighth Wind whispered:

"...winds evolve...

memory resists...

identity adapts...

and you... Seventh Wind...

are becoming uncontrollable..."

Kaelen's breath caught.

The Unheard whispered in terror:

"It fears you."

Kaelen stepped forward, eyes glowing.

"Then try to stop me."

The tear shuddered violently, its edges crackling like breaking glass.

The Eighth Wind hissed:

"...you will be unmade..."

And the limb lunged toward Kaelen.

V. The Clans Join the Fight — Unity for the First Time

Zephyr flicker-walkers grabbed Kaelen by the arms and pulled him aside as the limb tore through the air.

Tempestborn unleashed lightning—

the first strike that did not instantly die.

Sirocco flames surged—

burning bright even near the tear.

Mistral frost carved solid barriers—

slowing the distortion's advance.

Black Wisper assassins cast a silence-field—

forcing the Eighth Wind's whispers to weaken.

For the first time in history—

EVERY CLAN FOUGHT TOGETHER.

Kaelen shouted:

"STRIKE NOW—ALL WINDS TOGETHER!"
The clans converged in a storm of unity—
Wind, flame, frost, flicker, shadow, lightning—
All collided with the limb of the Eighth Wind.
The world exploded in light.
The tear buckled—
and shrank.
Not closed.
But weakened.
The limb withdrew.
The voice seethed:
"...you delay the inevitable..."
And with a final pulse, the tear sealed to a thin line.
The Eighth Wind retreated.
For now.

VI. Aftermath — Everyone Understands the Stakes

The clans stared at Kaelen, breathless and shaken.
Zephyr's commander whispered:
"That wasn't wind..."
Mistral's envoy whispered:
"That wasn't existence..."
Sirocco's sovereign whispered:
"That was the end."
Tempestborn stepped forward, placing a hand on Kaelen's shoulder.
"Seventh Wind...
what now?"
Kaelen looked at the thin scar in the sky.
It pulsed once.
A reminder.
A warning.
A promise.

Kaelen whispered:

"Now...

we prepare for war."

The Unheard looked at him.

"A war against the Architect?"

Kaelen shook his head.

"No."

He stared at the sky.

"A war against nothing itself."

Wind shivered across the plateau.

The clans felt destiny turn.

The world had one breath left.

7

"THE SIEGE OF WINDS"
Location: The Broken Amphitheater
Each Clan's Stronghold
Kaelen's personal training ground

The sky still bore the scar from the Eighth Wind's emergence — a thin white fracture that pulsed faintly like a heartbeat.

Everyone feared the moment it would pulse again.

The clans dispersed across the plateau, not in retreat, but in formation.

Each knew the battle ahead would be unlike any fought since the First Storm War.

The world was bracing itself.

For siege.

For annihilation.

For something that wasn't war, but the ending of breath.

I. Sirocco — The Burning Rampart

Sirocco's stronghold ignited with furious resolve.

Massive furnaces roared day and night.

Heatstorms carved trenches into the earth, creating rings of blistering protection.

The Scorched Sovereign oversaw it all, her eyes sharp with fear she refused to name.

"We do not fight wind," she declared.

"We fight death without flame.

Our heat must anchor existence."

Sirocco's warriors learned a new formation:

THE LIVING WALL

heat condensed into shields strong enough to resist unbreath for moments at a time.

Their motto changed today:

"OUR FIRE REMEMBERS."

Kaelen watched them from afar.

He whispered, "They're adapting."

The Unheard nodded.

"They must. Or they will vanish without even ash to mark their passing."

II. Mistral — The Frostbound Citadel

Mistral erected towering frost-ridges at the northern edge of the plateau.

Cold matter, infused with lineage memory, became anchors against identity erosion.

They believed something profound:

If the world forgets itself,

ancestry will remember.

Mistral elders etched ancient names into the ice:

Winds long dead

Stories long forgotten

Clans never recorded

A history the Eighth Wind could not erase

Their oath froze across the citadel walls:

"WE ENDURE BECAUSE WE REMEMBER."

Kaelen touched one ridge.

It pulsed back — steady and honest.

"These names... they're alive."

"Yes," the Mistral envoy said softly.

"And they stand with you."

III. Zephyr — The Shattered Mirage

Zephyr's flicker-walkers trained relentlessly, preparing for an enemy that defied time, distance, and form.

Their camp looked like a fracturing storm:

Blurs of motion.

Echoes of steps.

Shadows racing backward.

But within the chaos was precision.

They refined a technique that had only existed in theory:

THE MIRAGE BASTION

a wall made not of flame or frost

but of unpredictability

—motion so fragmented the Eighth Wind could not map it.

Zephyr's commander approached Kaelen.

"We cannot outrun the Hollow Wind," he said.

"But we can confuse it."

Kaelen nodded.

"You'll buy us time."

The commander smiled grimly.

"That's all we've ever done."

IV. Tempest — The Roaring Bulwark

Tempestborn stood at the center of a storm that spanned miles.

Thunder cloaked him like armor.

Lightning carved ancient sigils into the ground.

His army trained in the eye of the storm —

learning how to channel lightning inward,

to anchor their identities with electric imprint.

Their new creed:

"THE STORM REMEMBERS ITS NAME."

Kaelen entered the storm's edge.

Tempestborn met him, eyes crackling.

"You survived the Hollow Horizon," he said.

"I will survive the tear."

Kaelen held his gaze.

"You almost died when lightning failed."

Tempestborn nodded.

"Then I must learn to storm without wind."

He placed a hand on Kaelen's shoulder.

"I stand with you, Seventh Wind. Even if I fear you."

Kaelen smiled faintly.

"Fear keeps us honest."

V. Black Wisper — The Silent Veil

Black Wisper did not build walls.

They erased them.

Their stronghold became a veil of silence so complete that identity itself grew louder in contrast.

The Wisper elders gathered Kaelen into a ring of shadow.

"This is how silence survives," they whispered.

"By bending but never breaking."

Kaelen felt the silence settle into his bones.

"This... feels like armor."

"It is."

Their technique:

THE VEIL OF RETAINED SILENCE

which shields memories from the Eighth Wind's erasure.

The Wisper elder leaned close.

"Silence is not absence.

Silence is protection."

Kaelen bowed his head.

"I'll remember that."

VI. Kaelen — Training for the Final Confrontation

Kaelen walked alone to the plateau's center.

The sky fracture pulsed above.

He sat cross-legged, surrounded by seven winds and one memory deeper than all of them.

He whispered:

"I must evolve again."

The Unheard stood behind him.

"At what cost?"

Kaelen closed his eyes.

"The cost is irrelevant."

He placed one hand on the ground.

Identity hummed.

He placed the other hand on his heart.

Memory pulsed.

He exhaled—

And the Seventh Wind spiraled upward.

Threads of:

Concordia

Resonantia

Equalis

Sunder

Remembered Breath

Merged around him.

B ut something else stirred.
        A new pressure.
A new shape.
A new fear.
Kaelen whispered:
"I feel the Eighth Wind watching."
The Unheard nodded.
"It fears you."
Kaelen leaned forward, breath sharp.
"No... it's studying me."
A tremor ran through the sky fracture.
A whisper followed:
"...SEVENTH WIND..."
The Remembered Wind inside Kaelen surged.
Kaelen opened his eyes—
They glowed with threads of memory and flame and frost and silence and lightning all at once.
The Unheard whispered:
"You're becoming something else."
Kaelen nodded.
"I must."

VII. Foreshadowing: The Siege Will Be Tested

As the sun dipped beneath the plateau, every clan lit their defenses.

Sirocco firewalls erupted.

Mistral frost towers rose.

Zephyr mirage walls flickered.

Tempest storms coiled inward.

Black Wisper shadows deepened.

And Kaelen stood alone beneath the fracture.

The sky pulsed.

The wind shook.

The world inhaled.

Kaelen whispered:

"It begins soon."

The Unheard asked:

"The siege?"

Kaelen shook his head.

"No."

He looked up at the trembling fracture in the sky.

"The invasion."

8   "THE FIRST INVASION OF THE HOLLOW WIND"
Location: Sirocco's Burning Rampart
Edge of the Hollow Horizon's Expansion

Night fell without wind.
No breeze.

No whisper.

No shifting of air.

Just stillness.

The kind of stillness that pressed against the lungs, a warning from the world:

The Hollow Wind is coming.

Kaelen stood at the rampart with Sirocco's Scorched Sovereign, gazing toward the horizon where the sky fracture pulsed faintly like a heartbeat beneath the dark.

"It's testing us," Kaelen said.

The Sovereign's hands glowed with heat.

"We're ready."

Kaelen's jaw tightened.

"You're not."

The horizon flickered.

The Sovereign's eyes narrowed.

"What is that?"

Kaelen's breath hitched.

"That... is the first sign."

A faint line of pale light skittered across the ground like a crack spreading through glass.

Where it passed—

Sand turned grey.
Heat died.
Sound disappeared.
The Eighth Wind had made contact.

I. The Hollow Wind Arrives

The pale line pulsed—
and split open.
A silent explosion rippled outward.
Sirocco warriors were thrown off their feet—
not by force,
but by the absence of it.
Kaelen shouted:
"FORM THE LIVING WALL!"
Dozens of Sirocco warriors moved instantly, heat condensing
into a blazing barrier—
—but the flames sputtered.
Died.
Collapsed.
As if heat itself had been forgotten.
A Sirocco captain screamed:
"OUR FIRE IS—GONE—!"
Kaelen sprinted forward.
"Hold position! HOLD—"
CRACK.
A figure emerged from the pale rift.
Not humanoid.
Not wind.
Not shadow.
A distortion.
A wound in reality.
As it stepped forward, the air around it vanished—
wind collapsing inward,

heat extinguishing,

identity trembling.

The Eighth Wind had taken form.

The Unheard appeared at Kaelen's side, trembling.

"It's smaller than before," he whispered.

Kaelen shook his head.

"No.

It's focused."

The Architect was learning.

II. The Eighth Wind Searches for a Weakness

The distortion stopped.

It tilted—

as if listening.

As if smelling.

As if scanning the world for something.

Kaelen realized its intent instantly.

"It's looking for the clan with the weakest hold on identity."

The Unheard stiffened.

"No... not identity."

Kaelen's eyes widened.

"It's looking for lineage."

Because lineage was memory.

And memory was resistance.

The first to break were those whose breath carried the least ancestral anchoring.

Sirocco warriors.

Heat-born fighters lived in the moment.

Their lineage burned bright but brief.

The Eighth Wind had chosen its target.

III. Sirocco's Fall Begins

The distortion extended a limb of pale cancellation toward the Burning Rampart.

The nearest warrior screamed—

as his flame extinguished,
his identity flickered,
his memories dissolved,
and he collapsed into a blank silhouette.
Kaelen sprinted forward.
"NO!"
He pushed the Seventh Wind through him—
and slammed into the distortion's limb.
The world echoed with impact.
The limb recoiled slightly.
Kaelen staggered back.
The Scorched Sovereign screamed:
"SIROCCO! SHIELDS UP!"
But shields of fire died the moment they rose.
The Eighth Wind walked forward.
Each step erased heat from the world.
Furnaces dimmed.
Torches blinked out.
Entire trenches of molten sand cooled instantly.
Sirocco's domain was being silenced.

IV. The Clans Respond Too Late

Zephyr streaks flickered down from the sky.
Tempest lightning arced across the plateau.
Mistral frost rushed in waves.
Black Wisper shadows attempted to cloak the battlefield.
But none reached in time.
Kaelen shouted across the wind:
"HOLD THE FORMATIONS! DO NOT LET IT THROUGH—"
Zephyr's commander shouted back:
"WE AREN'T FAST ENOUGH—"
Tempestborn roared:
"THE STORM CAN'T FIND PURCHASE—"
Mistral's envoy gasped:

"Frost isn't forming—!"

Black Wisper's shadows writhed helplessly.

The Eighth Wind weakened everything around it—

including the bonds of memory the clans relied upon.

Kaelen's heart slammed.

Sirocco was standing alone.

V. Kaalen Attempts the Impossible

Kaelen inhaled deeply.

The Remembered Wind surged inside him, swirling like a storm of living memory.

The Unheard shouted:

"KAELEN—YOU CANNOT STAND AGAINST IT ALONE—"

Kaelen roared:

"I HAVE TO!"

He leapt.

The distortion turned its unseen face toward him.

Kaelen exhaled:

Remembered Wind — FULL CONCORDIA

A wave of luminous wind-patterns burst from his body—

threads of every wind entwined,

unified by memory,

reinforced by identity.

It struck the Eighth Wind—

And for a moment—

Just a moment—

The distortion hesitated.

Kaelen pushed harder—

every breath from every clan

every memory they carried

every name they had loved

every lineage they had sworn to protect

every wind that had ever lived

He forced all of it into a single strike.

The distortion split—
then reformed instantly.
Kaelen collapsed to one knee, coughing blood.
"Damn it—"
The Unheard dragged him back.
"It cannot be stopped alone!"
Kaelen looked up, defeated.
"Then Sirocco will fall."

VI. The Scorched Sovereign Makes Her Choice

The Sovereign stepped forward.

Her flames sputtered and died—

but her spirit did not.

She knelt beside Kaelen.

"Seventh Wind...

give me your memory."

Kaelen's eyes widened.

"What?"

"My fire dies," she said, voice steady.

"But my lineage does not.

Give me your memory—

and I will anchor Sirocco one last time."

Kaelen hesitated.

"It may kill you."

She smiled.

"What is death... compared to erasure?"

Kaelen placed his hand against her forehead.

The Remembered Wind surged into her.

Her eyes ignited with threads of memory—

IDENTITY

LINEAGE

ANCESTRY

PURPOSE

She rose.

Her body burned with memory-fire — flame made not of heat, but of history.

She walked toward the Eighth Wind—

Sirocco warriors kneeling behind her.

The distortion paused.

The Sovereign whispered:

"Fire is not heat.

Fire is remembrance."

She struck.

A column of memory-fire collided with the Eighth Wind's distortion.

The distortion recoiled—

folded—

rewound into itself—

and withdrew into the tear.

The sky fracture pulsed once.

The rift sealed.

Silence fell.

The world breathed again.

Sirocco had survived.

But as the Sovereign turned back toward her people—

Her memory-fire faded.

Her body flickered.

And she collapsed into Kaelen's arms.

Her final whisper:

"Protect... the winds..."

She dissolved into ashes of pure light—

a memory preserved

but a life ended.

Kaelen trembled.

The first casualty of the war against nothing—

was a Sovereign.

9 "THE SOVEREIGN'S ASHES"
Location: The Burning Rampart
The Ruins of Sirocco's Stronghold
The Central Amphitheater

The wind did not move.

Not even a whisper.

Sirocco's Burning Rampart — once a fortress of roaring flame and shifting heat — now stood dim, charred, and disturbingly cold.

Sirocco warriors knelt in the sand around a single mound of glowing embers.

The only remnants of their Sovereign.

Kaelen stood beside them, head bowed.

Her last ashes glimmered faintly with memory-fire — the residual echo of the Remembered Wind he had shared with her.

And because of that, Kaelen felt her final moments:

Her fear.

Her courage.

Her choice.

Her sacrifice.

Her hope for the world.

The Unheard hovered silently at Kaelen's shoulder.

Even he did not speak.

This was a moment for breath.

For memory.

For grief.

For consequences.

I. Sirocco Grieves — And Blames

A Sirocco captain approached Kaelen.

His voice shook.

"You gave her that power."

Kaelen nodded.

"I did."

"You let her burn alone."

Kaelen closed his eyes.

"She chose it. I didn't force—"

The captain snarled:

"SHE DID THAT TO PROTECT YOU!"

Silence cut through the rampart.

Mistral elders stiffened.

Zephyr flickers paused mid-step.

Tempestborn looked away.

Black Wisper shadows deepened.

Kaelen whispered:

"...I know."

The captain shoved him hard.

"You were supposed to stand with her!"

Sirocco warriors murmured in agreement—

anguish twisting into anger,

anger twisting into fear,

fear twisting into blame.

Kaelen didn't defend himself.

Didn't raise a hand.

Didn't summon wind.

Because the captain wasn't wrong.

Kaelen said softly:

"I should've been by her side."

The captain shouted:

"CAN YOU EVEN PROTECT US, KAELEN?!"

And that question

—that wound,

that truth—

echoed across the entire world.

II. The Clans Turn on the Seventh Wind (Not as Enemy, but as Fear)

Tempestborn stepped forward.

His voice was steady but hollow.

"You stopped the Eighth Wind's entry. But you couldn't stop its strike."

Kaelen nodded.

Zephyr's commander flickered beside him.

"You are stronger than any of us. But the Eighth Wind evolves faster than you can."

Kaelen's chest tightened.

Mistral's envoy looked at the glowing ashes.

"Our leaders cannot keep dying to buy us moments of survival."

Black Wisper whispered from the shadows:

"And you, Seventh Wind...

you are not immune."

Kaelen's hands trembled.

Because he knew they were right.

He had felt the Eighth Wind

inside his lungs,

inside his name,

inside his memories.

He whispered:

"...I'm not strong enough to face it alone."

This time, no one argued.

III. The Unheard Speaks the Truth No One Wants to Hear

The Unheard drifted forward, shadows rippling.

"Your Sovereign died a hero," he said gently.

"She did what no other leader would dare."

But his next words were sharper.

"But do not mistake her death as proof of Kaelen's failure.

The Eighth Wind is not something any wind can defeat alone."

Sirocco's captain spat:

"Then what is Kaelen for?"

The Unheard was silent for a moment.

Then:

"Kaelen is not a weapon.

He is a threshold.

A possibility the Architect fears."

Kaelen's breath stopped.

"What does that mean?"

The Unheard turned to him.

"You are not meant to defeat the Eighth Wind."

Sirocco growled.

Tempestborn clenched his fists.

Mistral looked horrified.

Zephyr paced anxiously.

Kaelen whispered:

"Then what am I meant to do?"

The Unheard answered:

"You are meant to become something the world has never seen."

IV. The Shadow Kaelen Arrives — And Makes Things Worse

The air rippled.

Kaelen's shadow stepped out of a fold in the wind—fractured, unstable, identity flickering like dying flame.

The clans drew their weapons instantly.

Kaelen raised a hand.

"No. Let him speak."

Sirocco hissed in fury.

But Kaelen's shadow only stared at the ashes of the Sovereign.

Then it whispered:

"She bought you minutes.
The Architect will take years."

Zephyr's commander stepped forward.

"Why come here, shadow?"

The shadow smiled faintly.

"To warn you."

Kaelen stiffened.

"Warn us of what?"

The shadow turned to Kaelen.

"The Eighth Wind chose Sirocco for one reason."

Kaelen's heart dropped.

"What reason?"

The shadow said:

"Because the next strike... will not be against a clan."

Kaelen whispered:

"...me."

The shadow nodded.

"The Architect has decided you must die before the invasion fully begins."

Sirocco erupted in panic.

Mistral stepped back.

Zephyr flickered involuntarily.

Tempestborn's lightning stuttered.

Black Wisper vanished into protective silence.

Kaelen felt the truth settle into him like cold stone.

He was the target.

The next strike would be personal.

V. Kaelen Breaks — Quietly, Finally

Kaelen walked away from the gathering, shoulders heavy, heart fractured.

He stared at the pale ashes of the Sovereign.

She had died because he wasn't fast enough.

Wasn't strong enough.

Wasn't enough.

He whispered:

"...I don't know if I can win this."

The Remembered Wind inside him flickered in distress.

The Unheard approached, quietly.

"Kaelen."

Kaelen didn't look up.

"I'm failing them."

"You're learning," the Unheard said gently.

Kaelen shook his head.

"People are dying because of me."

The Unheard's voice softened.

"No.

People are dying because the Architect has awakened."

Kaelen clenched his fists.

Tears rose—

not because of grief alone,

but because of fear.

Real, human fear.

He whispered:

"I am the Seventh Wind.

But I don't know what that means anymore."

The Unheard placed a hand on his shoulder.
"That is why the Architect fears you."
Kaelen looked up, confused.
The Unheard continued:
"You have not reached your final form."

VI.— The Ashes Speak

As Kaelen turned toward the rampart to leave—
The ashes of the Sovereign glowed.
A pulse of memory-fire.
A whisper rose from her remnants:
"Kaelen...
do not fear becoming."
Wind spiraled around the ashes—
not as flame,
but as living memory.
The Mistral envoy gasped:
"She's... blessing him."
Tempestborn bowed.
Zephyr flickered reverently.
Black Wisper lowered their shadows.
Kaelen stepped forward.
The ashes swirled around him—
wrapping him in threads of ancestral fire.
The Sovereign's final message echoed:
"Become what the world needs.
Not what it expects."
Kaelen inhaled.
The threads sank into him like embers into steel.
His breath steadied.
His eyes hardened.
His wind evolved—
not more powerful,
but more alive.

He whispered:
"I will not let your sacrifice be wasted."
The Unheard bowed.
The shadow watched silently.
A new wind stirred around Kaelen—
a proto-form of what he must eventually become.
The clans felt it.
The world felt it.
Even the sky fracture pulsed in reaction.
Kaelen turned to the horizon and said:
"Let the Eighth Wind come."
The siege
was over.
The war
had begun.

1^0 "THE HOLLOW TEMPEST"

Location: The Storm Barrens
Tempest Stronghold

The skies above the Storm Barrens boiled with lightning. Storm funnels spiraled across the horizon like coiled serpents.

Thunder rolled in relentless waves.

Electric sigils carved themselves into the stone by instinct alone.

This was Tempest territory.

Where storm obeyed

—and feared—

one man.

Tempestborn.

He stood at the center of a roaring vortex, arms outstretched, lightning crackling over his skin like molten silver.

He spoke softly into the storm:

"Do not break.

Not yet."

Because he could feel it approaching.

The Hollow Wind.

The Eighth Breath.

The thing that hunted Kaelen…

but had chosen him first.

I. The First Strike — Lightning Goes Silent

The sky fracture pulsed.

Lightning froze mid-air.

Not slowed.

Not interrupted.

Frozen.

Bolts stopped inches from the ground, trapped like insects in amber.

Tempestborn staggered.

"What—?"

His storm shrieked in silence.

Then

RRRRIP—

A pale line tore across the sky above the Barrens.

The Eighth Wind slid through like an idea slipping into a thought.

A distortion.

A wound.

A negation.

Tempestborn roared:

"FORM THE THUNDER WALL!"

Hundreds of Tempest warriors obeyed, lightning gathering into a circular bulwark—

—but the instant the Wall ignited—

the sparks vanished.

Electricity died.

Storm died.

Breath stuttered.

The Barrens fell silent.

A horror Tempest had never known.

11. Tempestborn Fights a Wind That Cannot Be Fought

The Eighth Wind extended a limb — a ripple of pale cancellation — toward the stronghold.

Stone dissolved.

Air collapsed.

Sigils erased themselves.

Tempestborn leapt into the air, summoning what storm he could.

He roared and struck with a bolt of pure will —

thunder that carried centuries of lineage behind it.

The bolt landed.

It fizzled into nothing.

Tempestborn's eyes widened.

"...it devours energy."

The distortion turned toward him, vibrating like a scream with no sound.

Tempestborn braced.

"I am the Storm," he growled.

"And storms do not kneel."

The limb struck him.

He was hurled through three stone ridges.

He rose, bleeding, breath unstable.

Still standing.

Still storm.

Kaelen would have been proud.

But the Eighth Wind did not relent.

It struck again.

Tempestborn blocked with arms glowing white-hot.

He was thrown a hundred feet.

He stood again.

Barely.

But the third strike—

broke him.

He fell to one knee, lightning bleeding from his skin in erratic sparks.

He whispered:

"...Kaelen...

you'd better hurry..."

Because he would not last much longer.

III. Kaelen Arrives — And Feels Fear for the First Time

Far across the plateau, Kaelen felt a jolt of pain through the Remembered Wind.

Kaelen gasped.

"Tempestborn!"

The Unheard's shadows shuddered.

"The Hollow Wind is at the Barrens."

Zephyr flickered into view, frantic.

"Mistral scouts report the storm has gone silent—"

Kaelen didn't wait.

He broke into a sprint, wind folding behind him.

"Kaelen!" the Unheard called out. "You aren't ready—!"

Kaelen snarled:

"I DON'T HAVE TIME TO BE READY!"

Lightning tore across the plateau as Kaelen accelerated.

Sirocco warriors watched him pass like a comet.

Wisper shadows parted before him.

Mistral bowed their heads.

Zephyr flickers raced to keep up and failed.

Kaelen soared into the Storm Barrens—

—and saw Tempestborn crawling to his feet, body cracking with dying electricity.

The Eighth Wind hovered above him, ready to erase him completely.

Kaelen's voice tore the sky:

"ENOUGH!"

The distortion turned.

Kaelen landed between it and Tempestborn.

Wind exploded outward.

The Eighth Wind's density bent around him.

Kaelen glared into the void.

"You want me?

Come take me."

The distortion hesitated.

Then lunged.

IV. Kaelen vs. The Hollow Wind (Round Two)

K aelen inhaled.
     The Remembered Wind spiraled around him.
  He exhaled a shockwave of unified breath:
REMEMBRANCE SHIELD
  The distortion hit the shield—
and buckled—
but did not break.
  Tempestborn dragged himself upright.
  "Kaelen... don't... let it touch you..."
  Kaelen nodded but didn't look back.
  "I won't."
  He thrust forward—
  SUNDER — The Breath That Breaks Fate
  Wind shattered on impact—
but the Eighth Wind simply absorbed the fragments.
  Kaelen staggered.
  "No good..."
  The Unheard appeared in a flicker of shadow.
  "Kaelen! You can't overpower it!"
  The Eighth Wind extended a second limb.
  It wrapped around Kaelen's arm.
  Kaelen screamed—

identity flickering,
memories tearing,
breath dissolving.

Tempestborn shouted:
"KAELEN!"
Kaelen roared and tore his arm free—
but a piece of his own name evaporated in the process.
He felt it.
A hollow space in his identity.
Fear.
Real fear.
This was the first time Kaelen understood:
The Eighth Wind could unmake him entirely.
And the next strike—
would hit Tempestborn.

V. Tempestborn's Last Storm

Tempestborn stumbled to Kaelen's side.
His eyes glowed faintly.
Lightning crawled across his skin like dying fireflies.
"Kaelen," he whispered.
"Let me stand with you."
Kaelen shook his head desperately.
"You can't fight it—"
Tempestborn smiled weakly.
"You once said fear keeps us honest.
Let me be honest now."
He raised his hands.
Lightning surged from the earth—
not stormborn lightning,
but identity lightning—
the electric memory of Tempest itself.
Tempestborn shouted:
"KAELEN! NOW!"

Kaelen understood instantly.

He inhaled—

and channeled Tempestborn's lineage lightning into the Remembered Wind.

Together, they struck.

Lightning of memory.

Wind of identity.

The strongest combined blow ever unleashed by two winds.

The distortion shuddered.

Folded.

Collapsed inward—

and retreated into the tear above the sky.

The Eighth Wind withdrew.

Not destroyed.

But stalled.

Tempestborn collapsed.

Kaelen caught him in his arms.

Lightning fizzled out.

Tempestborn smiled faintly.

"You... did well... Seventh Wind..."

Kaelen felt dread tightening in his throat.

"No. No, stay with me—"

Tempestborn placed a shaking hand against Kaelen's chest.

"Don't fear... becoming..."

Kaelen froze.

The same final words the Sovereign left him.

Tempestborn's eyes dimmed.

His lightning faded.

And the Storm of Tempest died.

In Kaelen's arms.

VI. The Aftermath — Two Leaders Fallen

When Kaelen carried Tempestborn's body into the amphitheater, the clans fell silent.

The Sirocco Sovereign was gone.

Now the Tempestborn had fallen too.

Two anchors.

Two titans.

Two leaders.

Gone.

Zephyr whispered:

"Two winds have died defending him…"

Mistral murmured:

"The Seventh Wind cannot protect us."

Black Wisper said nothing—

but their shadows curled in fear.

Kaelen lowered the body gently.

He whispered:

"I'm sorry."

The Unheard placed a hand on his shoulder.

"No.

You're transforming."

Kaelen clenched his fists.

"If I don't transform fast enough…

everyone will die."

The sky fracture pulsed overhead.

Kaelen glared at it with fury new to him.

He whispered to the Architect:
"You want me next?"
His wind surged.
"Come for me."
Wind trembled across the plateau.
The war was no longer approaching.
It had arrived.

1 [1] "THE UNRAVELING OF UNITY"

Location: The Central Amphitheater
One Day After Tempestborn's Death

The storm had been silent for 24 hours.
Not calmer.
Not gentler.
Silent — as if out of respect for its fallen master.
Two pillars of remembrance now stood in the amphitheater:
One of flame-glass for the Sirocco Sovereign.
One of storm-crystal for Tempestborn.
Both pulsed faintly with memory-wind, a reminder of what Kaelen had lost...
and what the clans had lost because of Kaelen.
Kaelen stood before the two pillars, head bowed.
The Unheard hovered behind him quietly.
Zephyr warriors flickered at the edges of the amphitheater, unable to stand still.
Mistral warriors huddled together, frost trembling on their armor.
Sirocco eyed the storm pillar with grief and bitterness.
Black Wisper shadows deepened into uneasy shapes.
And the shadow Kaelen stood at the back — watching everything unravel exactly as the Architect intended.

I. Sirocco's Accusation — The First Break

The Sirocco captain stepped forward.
"Two leaders dead," he said, voice trembling.
"Two titans gone.
Both died protecting Kaelen."
Kaelen felt the words hit him like blows.

The captain continued:

"How many more must burn for him?"

Mistral murmured in agreement.

Tempest warriors bowed their heads in mourning.

Zephyr flickers stopped moving entirely.

Kaelen spoke softly:

"I never asked them to die for me—"

"BUT THEY DID!" the captain roared.

His voice echoed across the amphitheater.

"You don't get to pretend their deaths aren't tied to you."

Kaelen swallowed hard.

"...I know."

The captain strode closer, pointing at Kaelen's chest.

"You said unity would save us.

All it's done is paint targets on our leaders."

Mistral's envoy stepped forward.

"We are not blind, Sirocco. Without Kaelen, the Eighth Wind would have consumed us all."

But Sirocco wasn't listening.

"Maybe.

But without Kaelen, the Architect might not have awakened in the first place."

Every clan froze.

Even the Unheard stiffened.

Kaelen felt as though the earth had dropped out beneath him.

"...You think this started because of me?"

Sirocco's captain didn't hesitate.

"I think the Architect woke because of YOU.

Because it sensed a wind that shouldn't exist.

Because it sensed a flaw in its world."

Kaelen took a step back.

The Mistral envoy whispered:

"That is... not impossible."

Zephyr flickered nervously.

Black Wisper whispered:

"It may be truth."

The amphitheater descended into murmurs:

"Kaelen is the catalyst."

"The Seventh Wind is the threat."

"We follow him into annihilation."

"He will bring the Eighth Wind down upon us all."

Kaelen felt the weight of every whisper like a blade.

II. Kaelen Tries to Speak — And Fails

Kaelen raised a trembling hand.

"Please. Listen to me—"

But Mistral's envoy stepped forward sharply.

"No. YOU listen."

Kaelen froze.

"You are powerful," the envoy said.

"But you are unstable.

You are changing too quickly for us to trust your evolution."

Zephyr added:

"You survived the Hollow Horizon, but you came back different."

Black Wisper whispered:

"You carry a wind we do not understand."

Sirocco's captain shouted:

"You ARE the Architect's target.

Which means you will put ALL OF US in its path!"

Kaelen's voice cracked.

"I'm trying to save you—"

Tempestborn's second-in-command stepped forward.

"And if you fail?

How many more Tempestborns will die?

How many more Sovereigns?"

Kaelen tried again.

"My goal is to protect the winds—"

But Sirocco cut him off.

"PROVE IT!"

Kaelen froze.

"Show us," Sirocco said.

"Show us you can protect us.

Show us you can stand between us and the Eighth Wind.

Show us you are not the flaw the Architect seeks to erase."

The amphitheater roared:

"PROVE IT!"

Kaelen breathed in—

and the Seventh Wind shook inside him.

He whispered:

"I... can't."

Silence fell instantly.

Total.

Horrified.

Paralyzing.

The clans stared at him with disbelief.

Kaelen whispered again, voice breaking:

"I can't promise that.

I don't know if I can protect everyone.

Or even myself.

I'm evolving, but I don't know what I'm becoming.

And I don't know when... or if... it will be enough."

His eyes dropped to the ground.

The amphitheater erupted.

"He admits he cannot save us."

"He IS the threat."

"We need another leader."

"We cannot follow the Seventh Wind into oblivion."

"We must remove him."

Kaelen's chest tightened.
Every breath in the amphitheater turned against him.
The Unheard stepped forward to defend him—
but Black Wisper's shadows blocked him.
Zephyr flickers formed a barrier.
Mistral frost surrounded their ranks.
Sirocco stoked new flames of anger.
Unity collapsed.
Completely.

III. The Architect Exploits the Fracture

The sky fracture pulsed.
A faint whisper rolled across the amphitheater:
"...division accelerates the unraveling..."
Kaelen staggered, clutching his head.
The Architect's voice slid into his breath:
"...you are alone now...
as you were meant to be..."
Kaelen gasped.
"NO—"
But the voice continued:
"...and soon, Seventh Wind...
you will be forgotten..."
Kaelen stepped back, shaking.
Black Wisper pointed.
"He hears it again."
Zephyr whispered:
"He's being influenced—"
Sirocco shouted:
"He's compromised!"
Mistral muttered:
"Maybe he belongs to the Hollow Wind already..."
Tempest's new commander whispered:
"Or maybe he is the Hollow Wind."

Kaelen opened his mouth—

But no wind formed the words.

IV. The Shadow Kaelen Speaks the Truth Kaelen Cannot

Kaelen's shadow stepped into the center of the amphitheater.

Every weapon rose instantly.

But the shadow raised a hand.

"Enough."

The clans froze at the sound of Kaelen's own voice—cold, clear, unshaken.

The shadow pointed to Kaelen.

"He is not your enemy."

Sirocco scoffed.

"And why should we trust you?"

The shadow smirked.

"Because I know exactly what he is becoming."

Kaelen's breath hitched.

"What... am I becoming?"

The shadow looked at him with something that almost resembled pity.

"You are becoming the one thing the Architect cannot erase."

Silence.

The shadow continued:

"But you cannot do it alone.
And they cannot do it divided."

He turned to the clans.

"He cannot prove himself yet.
Because he has not fully evolved."

Kaelen's heart slammed.

The shadow paused.

Then said the most important line of the chapter:

"You must decide whether to stand with a wind unfinished...
or die waiting for a wind that will never come."

The clans fell silent.

For the first time in the chapter—

they listened.

V. Kaelen Reclaims His Voice

Kaelen stepped forward.

His voice raw.

"I am not asking for faith.

I am asking for time.

Because the war is coming whether we unite or not."

Zephyr flickered uneasily.

Mistral shivered.

Sirocco glared.

Tempestborn's successor clenched his fist.

Kaelen continued:

"I will evolve.

I will stand between you and the Hollow Wind.

Even if you abandon me.

Even if you fear me.

Even if I die doing it."

He lifted his hand.

The Remembered Wind spiraled around him like luminous threads of ancestry, history, and identity.

"I don't expect you to trust me.

But I need you to breathe beside me."

Silence.

Then Zephyr flickered into a bow.

Mistral placed a fist to their chest.

Black Wisper lowered their shadows.

Tempestborn's successor nodded once.

Even Sirocco, bruised and grieving, bowed their heads.

Unity wasn't restored.

But it wasn't lost either.

Kaelen whispered:

"Thank you."

VI. A New Fracture Opens

The sky pulsed again.

A new fracture spread across the horizon.

Wider.

Brighter.

Hungrier.

The Architect whispered:

"...soon..."

Kaelen stared at the tear, breath slow and steady.

He whispered back:

"Not before I'm ready."

The Remembered Wind flared beside him.

The Unheard whispered:

"It's beginning again."

Kaelen nodded.

"And this time... it comes for me."

Wind shivered across the plateau.

The war had entered its final ascent.

1²   "THE FINAL THRESHOLD"
Location: The Fractured Plateau
Under the expanding sky-tear

Wind fled the plateau.
Not blew.
Not died.
Fled.

The air collapsed inward like the world was holding its breath.

The sky fracture, once a thin scar, now split wide across half the horizon—

a jagged rift of pale, devouring light that pulsed in slow, dreadful waves.

Every clan gathered on the plateau, arranged in defensive formations they knew would not hold.

Kaelen stood at the center.

The Remembered Wind coiled around him like threads of golden storm.

He looked up at the tear, chest tight, eyes bright with something between resolve and fear.

The Unheard whispered:

"It's pushing through."

Kaelen nodded.

"This time... it isn't sending a scout.
It's coming itself."

The sky pulsed.

RRRRRRRRRRIIIP—

The threshold ruptured.

And the Eighth Wind began to descend.

I. The Eighth Wind Takes Form

The clans braced—

but nothing could prepare them for the shape that emerged from the tear.

It wasn't a body.

It wasn't a storm.

It wasn't a shadow.

It was an absence of world made visible.

A humanoid silhouette of perfect stillness, carved from nothing.

No face.

No breath.

A hollow figure made of erased possibility.

But its presence made wind die, memory tremble, and identity collapse.

Tempestborn's successor whispered:

"...Creator help us..."

Sirocco's captain stepped back instinctively.

Mistral shivered as frost sublimated off their armor.

Zephyr flickers lost control and scattered.

Black Wisper shadows curled away in fear.

The Hollow Wind stepped forward.

Reality bent around its foot.

Stone dissolved.

Air folded inward.

Kaelen exhaled slowly.

"It's here."

II. Kaelen Steps Forward Alone

The clans formed a scattered semicircle behind him.

No one dared step closer.

Not even the Unheard.

Kaelen's shadow flickered beside him—

a fractured reflection of Kaelen's own fears.

But Kaelen stood tall.

"Architect!" he shouted, voice carrying across a dead wind.

"You want me?

I'm right here."

The Hollow Wind tilted its featureless head.

Then it spoke—

not in sound,

but in identity.

Kaelen heard it inside his bones:

"...you are an error..."

Kaelen clenched his fists.

"And yet... I still stand."

The Eighth Wind rippled.

"...you should not exist..."

Kaelen raised his chin.

"Then erase me."

The sky pulsed.

And the Hollow Wind obeyed.

III. The Architect Strikes — Reality Collapses

The Hollow Wind extended a limb—

a column of erasure.

Kaelen braced—

The Remembered Wind coiled—

But the strike didn't hit him.

It struck the ground in front of him.

And erased it.

A crater of pure nothingness expanded outward.
Sirocco warriors screamed as they fell back.
Zephyr flickers scrambled out of range.
Mistral frost shattered.
Tempest lightning failed instantly.

Kaelen realized the truth:

"It's not trying to erase me.
It's trying to erase EVERYTHING around me—
so there's nothing left for me to protect."

The Unheard shouted:

"KAELEN—MOVE!"

Kaelen did not.
He sprinted straight at the Hollow Wind.
Wind roared behind him.
The Remembered Breath flared like a rising sun.
Kaelen shouted:

"YOU WILL NOT ERASE THIS WORLD!"

And collided with the Hollow Wind.

IV. Kaelen vs. the Eighth Wind (Round Three)

The impact shredded reality.
Winds exploded in every direction.
Memory-fire spiraled.
Fragments of frost and lightning flickered into and out of existence.
Shadows warped into pure sound.

Kaelen was thrown back—
but he caught himself mid-air, twisting the Seventh Wind beneath him.

He landed and immediately launched forward again.
CONCORDIA — The Breath That Unifies
surged around him.

The Hollow Wind trembled slightly.
But just slightly.

Kaelen struck again with:
SUNDER — The Breath That Breaks Fate
The Hollow Wind absorbed the blow
and erased the fate Kaelen was trying to break.
Kaelen's chest heaved.
"This... thing is rewriting the rules."
The Hollow Wind lifted a limb.
"...you are not enough..."
Kaelen whispered:
"I know."
He activated:
RESONENTIA — The Breath That Hears Every Wind
Voices flooded into him—
Sirocco's fire lineage
Tempest's electric ancestry
Mistral's frozen history
Zephyr's fragmented breath
Wisper's eternal silence—
Kaelen roared:
"I am ALL winds!"
He struck.
For the first time—
the Hollow Wind staggered.
Just an inch.
Just a moment.
But it staggered.
The clans watched in awe.
But the Hollow Wind straightened.
Then it whispered:
"...then become all winds...
and break with them..."
Kaelen's blood went cold.
The Architect wasn't trying to kill him.

It was trying to push him into evolution—
so it could erase him at his peak.

V. The Hollow Wind's Full-Entry Attempt

The tear widened behind the Hollow Wind.
Light vanished from the sky.
Colors washed out.
Sound flattened.
The plateau began dissolving from the edges inward.
Sirocco's captain screamed:
"THE WORLD IS COLLAPSING!"
Mistral elders shouted:
"It's consuming the horizon!"
Zephyr's commander yelled:
"KAELEN! STOP IT!"
Kaelen sprinted forward—
but the Hollow Wind flicked a limb outward.
Kaelen froze mid-step.
Literally froze.
Not paralyzed.
Frozen in identity-stasis.
His memories flickered.
His breath stuttered.
His name evaporated—
for a heartbeat.
The Unheard gasped:
"It's overwriting him!"
Kaelen struggled—
The Remembered Wind screamed inside him—
And with a roar, he broke free.
But every clan saw it.
Kaelen was vulnerable.
The Hollow Wind tilted its head.
"...you cannot stop my arrival..."

Kaelen wiped blood from his mouth.

"No."

He inhaled.

Wind spiraled around him, deep and luminous.

"But I can stall it."

He slammed his hands into the ground.

DIVISIO — The Breath That Separates Truth From Lie activated—

splitting the plateau into layers of real and unreal.

The tear froze.

The Hollow Wind paused.

For the first time—

Kaelen had stalled a full-entry.

But only stalled.

Not stopped.

The Hollow Wind whispered:

"...you delay... nothing more..."

Kaelen stood tall.

"That's all I need."

The Eighth Wind pulsed.

The plateau cracked.

Kaelen stared into the void.

"Come on then."

He roared:

"COME THROUGH ME!"

VI. The Threshold Holds... For Now

The Hollow Wind pushed—

Kaelen pushed back—

The threads of the Seventh Wind flared like burning constellations—

And the tear stopped widening.

Just barely.

Just temporarily.

But it stopped.
Kaelen collapsed to one knee.
Breath shaking.
Identity trembling.
The Hollow Wind retreated one step.
Not defeated.
Not afraid.
Calculating.
The Architect whispered:
"...you evolve...
and so must I..."
Kaelen's eyes widened.
The tear dimmed.
The Hollow Wind stepped backward into it—
but its final whisper chilled the world:
"...next time...
I will not come alone..."
The tear sealed to a thin line.
Kaelen fell forward, catching himself on shaking arms.
The clans rushed forward.
The Unheard held him upright.

Zephyr whispered:
"You held it back…"
Mistral added:
"…but for how long?"
Sirocco said nothing.
Black Wisper whispered:
"The next threshold will break."
Kaelen stared at the horizon.
Whispered:
"No.
I won't let it."
But his voice trembled.
Because even he didn't know if he believed that anymore.

1³ "THE LAST BREATH BEFORE WAR"

Location: The Plateau of Convergence

Nightfall

Wind barely moved.
Not from calm—
but from fear.
The sky fracture had shrunk back to a faint scar,
yet every clan felt the truth:
The Architect had not retreated.
It had recalculated.
The Hollow Wind would return
not as one
—but as many.
Kaelen stood alone on the highest ridge overlooking the plateau.
He was trembling.
He did not hide it.
The Seventh Wind flickered around him—
weaker than before,
yet somehow more focused.
Like a blade chipped at the edges
but honed at the core.
The Unheard appeared behind him.
"Kaelen," he said softly,
"the clans are gathering."
Kaelen nodded.
He took one breath—
long, deep, steady.
The last breath of Book One.

Then he walked toward the waiting clans.

I. The Clans Assemble — Broken, United, Afraid

The amphitheater was full.

No one spoke.

Sirocco's warriors stood with faces of flame and grief.

Mistral formed walls of frost, steady but shaken.

Zephyr flickers moved in anxious patterns.

Tempest fighters carried stormless weapons.

Black Wisper shadows clustered silently, heavier than ever.

Two memorial pillars glowed side by side:

Sovereign

Tempestborn

The air around them hurt.

Kaelen walked between the pillars—

feeling both blessings and accusations

press into him with every step.

Sirocco watched with hatred and heartbreak.

Mistral watched with wary hope.

Zephyr watched with fear.

Tempest watched with emptiness.

Black Wisper watched with unreadable silence.

Kaelen stepped into the center.

I. Kaelen Speaks His Truth (The First Rally)

Kaelen's first words were not strong.
They did not echo.
They did not command.
They simply were.
"I can't promise survival."
A ripple of shock ran through the clans.
Kaelen continued:
"I can't promise victory.
I can't promise unity.
I can't promise that I won't fail."
Sirocco scowled.
Mistral winced.
Zephyr held their breath.
Kaelen raised his chin.
"But I can promise this—"
Wind spiraled around him.
"I will not run."
He stepped forward.
"I will not hide."
Wind intensified.
"I will not surrender to the Hollow Wind."
The Seventh Wind snapped outward
—not bright,
not powerful,
but alive.

Kaelen closed his fist.

"And I will evolve until I either break...

or become what this world needs."

Silence.

Then Zephyr flickered into a bow.

Mistral lowered their frost in acknowledgment.

Wisper shadows rippled with respect.

But Sirocco's captain glared.

"You say that," he snapped,

"but the Architect is evolving faster than you."

Tempest warriors murmured in agreement.

Kaelen nodded.

"That's why I need all of you."

He raised his hand.

"We go to war together.

Or we die alone."

II. The Strategic Divide (A Quiet Collapse)

The clans formed a circle around Kaelen.

This was supposed to be a unity council.

It became something else.

Mistral spoke first:

"If the Architect sends multiple Hollow Winds, our frost walls will collapse instantly."

Zephyr added:

"We cannot outmaneuver a wind that erases the map."

Tempestborn's successor shook his head.

"And without Tempestborn, the storm is... unanchored."

Sirocco growled:

"Then why follow Kaelen? Why not choose a new vanguard?"

Kaelen stiffened.

The Unheard stepped forward sharply.

"Because the Seventh Wind is the only wind the Architect fears."

Sirocco spat:

"Or the only wind it wants to erase."

Black Wisper whispered:

"Both can be true."

The amphitheater erupted.

Anger.

Fear.

Accusations.

Despair.

The fragile unity Kaelen rebuilt in Chapter Eleven began cracking again.

Kaelen closed his eyes.

He whispered to himself:

"I can't hold them together..."

Then—

The sky fracture pulsed.

A ripple of hollow light swept across the plateau.

Every clan fell silent.

Every head turned upward.

IV. The First Sign — The Tear Splits

The sky fracture trembled.

Then—

CRRRRRAACK—

A second fracture opened beside it.

Shorter.

Sharper.

Hungrier.

Sirocco gasped:

"A new tear—"

Zephyr whispered:

"Oh no..."

Mistral shivered.

Black Wisper shadows recoiled.

Kaelen's heart dropped.

"...multiple thresholds."

The Unheard nodded grimly.

"The Architect is dividing itself."

Kaelen froze.

"That means—"

The Unheard finished:

"It's creating more Hollow Winds."
Fear spread like wildfire.
Tempestborn's successor shouted:
"We can't fight many—"
Sirocco snapped:
"We can't even fight one—"
Zephyr panicked:
"We need to retreat—"
Mistral's envoy trembled:
"We need to hide—"
Kaelen stepped forward.
"NO."
Wind snapped outward.
Raw.
Instinctive.
Commanding.
The amphitheater froze.
Kaelen spoke with a voice deeper than wind:
"We don't run.
We prepare."

V. Kaelen's First Vision — The 8th Prophecy

The Seventh Wind flickered wildly around Kaelen.
His eyes rolled back.
He collapsed to one knee—
and a vision swallowed him whole.
The clans watched helplessly as Kaelen's body convulsed.
Inside the vision, Kaelen saw:
· A city made of storms frozen mid-breath.
· Zephyr flicker-walkers erased mid-step.
· Sirocco's flames extinguished across endless dunes.
· Mistral citadels melted into white dust.
· Black Wisper's shadows turned inside-out.
And at the center:

Multiple Hollow Winds stepping out of multiple tears.
Not one Architect.
But an army of stillness.

Kaelen screamed.
The Remembered Wind flared violently.
He saw a final image:
A silhouette of himself—
but older,
brighter,
more complete—
standing against the Architect's legion.

Then—
A whisper:
"Become the Ninth Wind."
Kaelen's breath stopped.
He collapsed forward into consciousness.

VI. The Prophecy Kaelen Cannot Ignore

The clans rushed to him.
The Unheard held him upright.
"What did you see?"
Kaelen trembled.
"I saw... the future."
Sirocco snarled:
"Then tell us!"
Kaelen lifted his head.
"The Architect won't send one Hollow Wind.
It will send many.
War is coming in waves."

Silence.
Then Kaelen added the line that reshaped the entire series:
"And I...
I must become more than the Seventh Wind."

Mistral's envoy whispered:

"More...?"

Zephyr flickered anxiously.

Sirocco shook their head.

Black Wisper shadows pressed closer.

Kaelen closed his eyes.

"I must become something that has never existed.
Something between life and erasure.
Between identity and stillness.
Between wind and unbreath."

He whispered:

"I must become the Wind That Stands Against Nothing."

The Unheard froze.

"...the Ninth Wind."

VII. The Cliffhanger

The sky pulsed with both fractures.
Two tears.
Two thresholds.
Two incoming Hollow Winds.
Kaelen stepped forward, breath steady.
The world watched him.
"The Architect is coming," he said.
He lifted his hand.
Wind spiraled upward—
not bright,
not pure,
but evolving.
"I won't be ready."
He turned toward the clans.
"Not by myself."
He pointed at each clan in turn:
"Sirocco.
Mistral.
Tempest.
Zephyr.
Wisper."
"We stand together now—
or we fall one by one."
No one replied.
Their fear was too great.

Kaelen inhaled—
and the Seventh Wind throbbed with ancient memory.
"For the last time in this book," he whispered:
"Stand with me."
Wind flared.
The sky fractures glowed.
And then—
BOOOOM—
Both tears burst open at once.
Two Hollow Winds stepped through.
Kaelen's whisper:
"...it begins."

Part IV

1 "THE LAST BREATH BEFORE WAR – CONTINUED"
Location: The Barrens

Moments After Kaelen Repels the Tempestborn

Stormbreaker Fang's roar cracked across the dunes as lightning stitched violently through the clouds. His storm tried to rebuild itself through instinct alone — but Kaelen felt it trembling.

Lightning feared him now.

Fang lowered his stance, chest heaving, armor ringing with unstable thunder.

"Seventh Wind..." he growled, "...you are bending storms that do not belong to you."

Kaelen took one step forward.
Wind spiraled around his ankles — not chaotic, not broken — *focused*.

"I'm not bending anything," he said.
"I'm choosing."

The Unheard drifted between them, shadows shaking in a way Kaelen had never seen.
"Tempestborn," he warned, "if you strike again, his evolution will force him to respond in kind."

Fang spat lightning into the dirt.
"He is already responding in kind!"

He hurled his spear — a solid bar of storm-forged will.

Kaelen didn't dodge.

He inhaled.

DIVISIO flared.

Stormbreaker Fang's attack split in mid-air — one half dissolving harmlessly into sand, the other half freezing in front of Kaelen like a suspended thought.

The battlefield went silent.

Kaelen exhaled lightly — and the suspended spear disintegrated into motes of wind and memory.

Fang stared at him in disbelief.

"What *are* you becoming?"

Kaelen didn't answer at first.

His own breath felt heavier, older — as though the winds of a thousand forgotten names were pushing at the edges of his bones.

"I'm becoming," he said finally, "what the world needs more than what the clans want."

The sky flickered.

Every clan felt it.

A ripple of hollow pressure trembled under the sand, humming like a breath pulled from the world itself.

Fang stepped back, eyes narrowing.

"...the Hollow Wind is watching."

Kaelen nodded.

"It's waiting for one of us to fall."

The Unheard whispered sharply:

"No. Not one. It's waiting for the *clans* to break."

The three of them froze.

Because cracks had already begun to spread across the horizon — faint, hairline fractures in the air itself — reacting to every heartbeat of division.

Fang swallowed hard.

"Then our fighting feeds it."

Kaelen's voice dropped.

"Yes."

For the first time, the Tempestborn hesitated.

Lightning dimmed.

The storm around him softened, uncertain.

Kaelen lowered his hand.

"Stormbreaker Fang... the war between us is a distraction. The Hollow Wind will return with more than one voice. More than one shape. It will bring *echoes*."

Fang clenched his jaw.

"And if those echoes come wearing the faces we trust?"

Kaelen stepped forward.

"Then I will separate truth from lie."

The Unheard bowed his head.

"The Second Ability is awakening fully."

A deep rumble rolled beneath them — a warning pulse from the bones of the world.

Fang inhaled sharply, understanding the message before Kaelen spoke it:

"The next threshold is opening," Kaelen whispered.

"And this time... it isn't opening in the sky."

He pointed behind Fang.

The Tempestborn turned — and his eyes widened.

A thin, vertical seam glowed across the desert floor, stretching like a wound tearing open the earth.

A **ground-entry**.

Something even Primordial Winds considered impossible.

Kaelen felt his heart pound.

"The Hollow Wind," he murmured, "is learning."

The seam widened.

A second whisper drifted out — softer than dust, older than truth.

"...Seventh Wind...

...your reflection was only the first of us..."

The Unheard went rigid.

Kaelen whispered:

"No..."

Fang tightened his grip on what remained of his shattered storm.

"What comes through now?" he asked.

Kaelen's breath trembled.

"Not a shadow."

He stepped back.

"An echo."

Wind spiraled violently as the seam split open —

And a figure stepped out.

Not Kaelen.

Not a clan warrior.

Not a Primordial shape.

Something wearing the *echo* of Kaelen's first breath — the exact moment the Seventh Wind touched human form.

A version of him he had never been.

A version of him that might have been.

A version of him that the Hollow Wind wanted to weaponize.

The echo smiled gently.

"...Kaelen...

...I remember you..."

Kaelen's blood ran cold.

Because the echo's voice was not a threat.

It was tender.

Affectionate.

A memory he did not have.

A memory that should not exist.

Stormbreaker Fang whispered:

"What is it?"

Kaelen exhaled — slow, terrified.

"That..." he said,

"...is my first breath."

The echo stepped forward.

The threshold behind it pulsed.
And the war finally began.

2 "THE FIRST BREATH ECHOES"
Location: The Barrens
Direct Continuation

The echo moved with unbearable calm — no flicker, no distortion, no corruption.

Its breath didn't waver.

Its steps didn't tremble.

Its presence did not fracture reality the way the shadow had.

This one was perfect.

Too perfect.

Kaelen's chest tightened.

This is what I would have been... if I were born human.

The echo stopped an arm's length away, studying Kaelen with the quiet curiosity of a child seeing sunlight for the first time.

"You learned to stand," it whispered.

"You learned to breathe.

You learned to choose."

Kaelen staggered back.

Stormbreaker Fang's hand shot out in front of him, lightning snaking across his gauntlet.

"Echo or not," he growled, "you step closer and I erase you."

The echo tilted its head — the gesture soft, almost innocent.

"You cannot erase something that never lived."

The Unheard shivered.

"Kaelen," he whispered, "this is not a construct. Not a mimic. Not a stolen memory."

Kaelen swallowed.

"I know."

The echo closed its eyes.

Wind swirled around it — gentle currents, warm and bright, filled with the scent of a world before the Fracture.

"I am your unclaimed destiny."

Kaelen felt his breath stutter.

"What does that mean?"

The echo opened its eyes.

It was like looking into a version of himself that had never touched pain.

Never tasted fear.

Never carried the weight of seven winds or the expectations of clans desperate for salvation.

"I am what you were supposed to become," it said, "before choice altered you."

Fang's lightning cracked sharply.

"Choice?" he barked. "What choice?!"

The echo's gaze slid to him — almost pitying.

"The moment Kaelen chose to remember, he diverged from me."

Kaelen's heart hammered.

"My memory... changed my evolution?"

The echo nodded.

"You embraced identity.

You embraced burden.

You embraced the winds that defined you — even when it broke you."

The sand around them vibrated with rising pressure.

The Unheard hissed:

"The Hollow Wind sent this.

To show you what you could have been."

"No," the echo whispered gently, "I came because he is un-prepared."

Kaelen stiffened.

"For what?"

The echo's face changed —

a flicker of sorrow,

a flicker of admiration,

a flicker of something like mourning.

"For the moment all versions of you must meet."

Fang's voice dropped.

"...there are more?"

The ground split again — just a thin line, but deep enough to bleed pale wind into the air.

Kaelen felt six distinct pulses echo through his bones.

Not one reflection.

Not one memory.

Not one echo.

But six.

ach pulse carried a version of Kaelen shaped by a different wind-path:

· **A Kaelen who embraced pure storm**
· **A Kaelen who surrendered to silence**
· **A Kaelen who fractured his name**
· **A Kaelen who never accepted flesh**
· **A Kaelen who followed the Architect**
· **A Kaelen who rejected all winds and became void**

Each pulse carried a future that could have been — or might still be.

Fang took a step back.

"Seventh Wind... what have you done?"

Kaelen shook his head.

"I didn't do this."

The echo touched his arm — gently, as if steadying him.

"This is not punishment," it whispered.

"This is convergence."

Kaelen stared at the widening seam.

"What does convergence mean?"

The echo breathed in — slowly, reverently.

"It means the Hollow Wind will not choose which version of you enters its domain."

Its eyes lifted to the sky.

"It will choose the strongest."

The seam split open.

Wind screamed.

Six silhouettes rose from the fracture below — each carrying a different face of Kaelen, each shaped by a path he never walked.

The echo stepped back.

"This is the trial that decides the war."

Kaelen felt his breath break inside his chest.

"What trial?"

The echo smiled softly, sadly, beautifully.

"The trial," it whispered,

"to decide which Kaelen survives the end of the world."

"THE SIXTH CONVERGENCE"
Location: The Barrens

N ow Splitting into Six Pathways
Wind detonated outward as the seam tore fully open.
The sky buckled.
The dunes folded.
Reality stuttered.
Kaelen braced himself—
—but every version of him rising from the fracture stood effortlessly, as if the world moved *around* them instead of the other way around.
Six silhouettes.
Six breaths.
Six destinies.
All rooted in him.
All diverged from him.
All arriving for him.
The Unheard staggered, shadows thrashing like cornered animals.
"Kaelen—this is forbidden. Even the Primordials never faced their own divergences."
Stormbreaker Fang planted his spear, lightning surging in defensive arcs.
"You expect him to fight *himself* six times?"
The echo — the gentle one — floated upward, eyes glowing softly.
"No.
He must understand them."

I. The First Divergence — The Stormborn Kaelen

The first silhouette stepped forward, armored in living thunder.

Lightning crawled across his veins like ancestral tattoos.

His voice cracked the dunes:

"I am the Kaelen who embraced storm over memory.

I am certainty.

I am wrath shaped into breath."

He raised a hand.

The sky obeyed.

Lightning spiraled into a crown above him.

Fang's jaw dropped.

"That... that is a Tempest Sovereign. But stronger."

The Stormborn Kaelen pointed at the real Kaelen.

"You failed the storm.

You hesitated.

I do not."

The ground around him fused into glass under sheer voltage.

Kaelen clenched his fists.

"I didn't choose storm. I chose balance."

"And that," Stormborn growled,

"is why you're weak."

II. The Second Divergence — The Silent Kaelen

The next silhouette stepped forward without sound.

No wind.

No presence.

No breath-trace at all.

Black Wisper warriors would have bowed to him as a Sovereign.

His eyes were depthless voids, absorbing every motion, every heartbeat.

"I am the Kaelen who surrendered entirely to silence."

His whisper erased a dune behind him.

Not flattened.

Not shifted.

Erased.

The Unheard trembled — truly trembled.

"That is Silence Absolute... something even Wisper abandoned ages ago."

Silent Kaelen tilted his head at the real Kaelen.

"You speak too much truth.

You reveal too many lies.

If you walked my path...

the world would have no lies left to tell."

III. The Third Divergence — The Fractured Kaelen

This one emerged in broken flickers.

Half-steps.

Half-gestures.

Reality unwilling to hold him still.

He was Zephyr without restraint — speed without identity.

"I am the Kaelen who refused a stable name.

I fractured myself to escape fate."

He moved —

and appeared behind Kaelen instantly.

Kaelen flinched.

Fractured Kaelen smiled.

"You carry too much weight.

Break, and you will be free."

IV. The Fourth Divergence — The Breathless Kaelen

The fourth figure hovered above the ground, flesh dissolving into raw wind.

Pure Seventh Wind.

No human form at all.

"I am the Kaelen who rejected the vessel your mother gave us."

His voice echoed through the dunes, layered, formless.

"I abandoned body.

You cling to it."

Kaelen's pulse froze.

This one felt closest to the Eighth Wind.

Too close.

V. The Fifth Divergence — The Architect's Kae-len

The fifth climbed out slowly, each step cracking the ground.

His eyes glowed the pale unbreath of the Hollow.

Not corrupted.

Chosen.

"I am the Kaelen who accepted the Architect's offer.

I am purpose without resistance.

I am clarity without burden."

The sand around him dissolved into pale dust.

Stormbreaker Fang roared:

"ABOMINATION!"

Architect's Kaelen didn't look at him.

He looked only at the real Kaelen.

"You think choice makes you strong.

Choice weakens you.

Join me, and none of us have to die."

VI. The Sixth Divergence — The Void Kaelen

The final silhouette didn't rise.

It *grew* — emerging like a shadow cast by a world that didn't exist anymore.

Tall.

Hollow.

Face blurred except for two white pinpoints of non-light.

When it spoke, the dunes dimmed.

"I am the Kaelen who rejected all winds.
All prophecy.
All fate."
Void filled the air around him.
"I chose nothing.
And nothing chose me."
The echo beside them — the gentle Kaelen — whispered in horror:
"This one should not exist."
The Void Kaelen lifted a hand.
The world groaned.

VII. Convergence Begins

The six divergences stood in a circle, each facing the real Kaelen.
Stormborn thundered:
"Only one path survives the end."
Silent erased another dune.
"To choose wrong is to destroy truth."
Fractured flickered around Kaelen, unreadable.
"Break or be broken."
Breathless whispered like a dying storm.
"You cannot win with a body."
Architect's Kaelen smiled.
"You cannot win with a conscience."
Void Kaelen extended his hand.
"Choose... or I will choose for you."
The real Kaelen inhaled.
The Seventh Wind swirled within him — weak, damaged, trembling — but still his.
Still the wind that remembered.
"I won't choose," Kaelen said.
"I will understand."
All six divergences spoke simultaneously:

"You don't have that long."
The fracture beneath them pulsed — widening, hungering.
The Hollow Wind was listening.
Waiting.
Choosing.

4   "THE FIRST CLASH — STORM VS. MEMORY"

The six divergences tightened their circle around Kaelen.

Sand spiraled upward from the pressure of their competing breaths.

Stormbreaker Fang braced himself, lightning swirling around his gauntlets.

The Unheard whispered:

"They're testing you.

One at a time at first...

because even your shadows don't understand what you are now."

Kaelen didn't respond.

His eyes never left the six alternate selves.

A single crack of thunder snapped the silence.

Stormborn Kaelen stepped forward.

Lightning crowned him.

Storm-will radiated from every movement.

The sky bent toward him as if the storm itself recognized its master.

He raised an arm toward the real Kaelen.

"Your first test is simple," he said.

A heartbeat passed.

"Survive."

I. The Stormborn Charges

Stormborn vanished in a streak of white-blue voltage.

Fang barely had time to shout—

"KAELEN, MOVE—!"

—but the strike already landed.

Lightning ripped across the barrens.

Sand vitrified into glowing glass.

Wind recoiled in spirals of pain.

Kaelen flew backward, slammed into a dune, and sank halfway into molten sand.

His bones rang.

His breath fractured.

His thoughts stuttered.

Stormborn appeared above him, floating on pillars of thunder.

"You feel that?" he said calmly.

"That is the storm you refused to become."

Kaelen coughed, smoke leaving his lungs.

"You confuse power with identity."

Stormborn extended a hand.

"You confuse restraint with weakness."

A bolt of sovereign-level lightning flashed—

—but Kaelen rolled aside as it detonated the dune.

Stormborn didn't chase.

He didn't need to.

The storm itself attacked — sand turning to spears of glass, air turning to sonic booms, lightning turning to whips that herded Kaelen into a tightening death-circle.

Kaelen raised an arm.

Seventh Wind flickered weakly.

Too weak.

Stormborn saw it.

"You're fragmented," he said.

"And fragmented beings don't win storms."

He raised both hands.

The sky turned black.

Fang stumbled backward in awe.

"That's a *supercell*. He's forming a living supercell!"

The Unheard whispered, horrified:

"He's drawing from the Tempestborn Sovereign oath. Access that Kaelen never took."

Stormborn's thunder rolled across the barrens like a god inhaling.

"Kaelen," Stormborn said,

"this is mercy."

He dropped the sky.

II. Kaelen Takes the Strike

Thunder crushed the world.

Lightning didn't strike — it *fell*, a pillar thick as a tower.

Kaelen vanished inside the storm.

Sand spiraled upward.

The ground split open.

Hollow wind shuddered at the force.

Fang roared:

"KAELEN!"

The storm raged for seven heartbeats—

Then silence.

Stormborn lowered his hands.

The supercell faded.

"I don't take pleasure in your death," he said softly.

"I take duty."

He turned—

—and froze.

Because something inside the crater shifted.

Something breathing.

Something glowing.

Kaelen rose slowly, smoke pouring from his body.

The Seventh Wind rippled around him — still weak, still fractured — but now refusing to extinguish.

Stormborn's eyes narrowed.

"...impossible."

Kaelen wiped blood from his lip.

"I survived."

"HOW?" Stormborn snapped.

Kaelen looked him dead in the eyes.

"You forgot what my wind is."

He stepped forward.

"I don't erase."

Another step.

"I don't mimic."

Another step.

"I don't fracture."

Lightning cracked in alarm as Stormborn retreated a half step.

Kaelen's voice deepened, resonant:

"I remember."

III. The Seventh Wind Awakens a New Layer

Kaelen inhaled.

Not deeply.

Not forcefully.

Just deliberately.

Wind unfurled around him — not loud, not violent, but *absolute*.

A memory-wind.

Warriors on distant cliffs felt ancestors stir.

Zephyr scouts felt forgotten footsteps echo.

Mistral envoys felt frost from generations long dead.

Sirocco fighters felt the warmth of their first campfires.

Stormborn felt something he had never felt:

A storm surrender.

Not out of defeat.

Out of recognition.

Kaelen spoke:

"You are the storm I could have become.
But storms forget their purpose."
Stormborn growled, lightning sharpening—
"And what purpose do you think storms serve?"
Kaelen exhaled.
The Seventh Wind flowed outward—
—and every crack of lightning on Stormborn's body dimmed.
"Storms warn," Kaelen said softly.
"Storms teach.
Storms cleanse."
He stepped directly into Stormborn's storm-field.
"And storms stop when the world cannot bear more."
Stormborn trembled.
Lightning stuttered across his body like a heartbeat misfiring.
"What... are you doing to me?"
The Unheard whispered:
"He's using Divisio—not on lies, but on excess. He's separating the storm from the rage."
Kaelen placed a hand on Stormborn's chest — inches from lightning, heat, and death.
Stormborn froze.
Kaelen whispered:
"You're not my enemy.
You're my warning."
He lowered his hand.
Stormborn staggered backward, lightning collapsing into harmless sparks.
His voice shook for the first time:
"...I lost control?"
Kaelen nodded.
"We all do."
Stormborn looked away — ashamed, confused, disarmed.
"Then I failed my test."

Kaelen shook his head.

"No.

You passed."

Stormborn blinked.

"How?"

Kaelen stepped back as the Seventh Wind pulsed around him.

"Because you reminded me that evolution without restraint becomes destruction."

Stormborn bowed his head — not in submission, but in respect.

"Then face the next of us," he said.

He stepped aside.

IV. The Silent Kaelen Steps Forward

The air vanished.

Sound vanished.

Wind vanished.

Even breath felt optional.

The Silent Kaelen floated forward, a shadow of stillness wearing Kaelen's face.

He raised one finger.

The dunes died.

The world dimmed.

And Kaelen felt his voice tear away.

The Silent Kaelen whispered:

"Now speak without words, Seventh Wind."

5   "THE SECOND CLASH
SILENCE VS. TRUTH"

S ilence flooded the barrens.
 Not absence—
but presence.

A crushing, total, suffocating presence.

The Silent Kaelen hovered inches above the sand, his form wrapped in a void so perfect not even shadows dared approach. Every breath within a hundred paces simply... stopped choosing to exist.

Stormbreaker Fang fell to one knee, clutching his throat.
The Unheard froze, eyes wide—silence was his domain, but this was beyond mastery.
Beyond technique.
Beyond wind.

"Kaelen..." the Unheard mouthed, voice trapped in the void between moments, "...be careful..."

Only Kaelen heard the faintest echo of the warning.

The Silent Kaelen pointed a single finger toward him.

The world muted.

Kaelen felt his breath compress—not by force, but by *permission*.
Silence demanded he stop breathing.
Silence demanded stillness.
Silence demanded surrender.

The Silent Kaelen spoke without speaking:

"Words distort truth."

Kaelen's pulse faltered.

"Breath distorts intention."

His ears rang with the lack of sound.

"Silence reveals everything."

Kaelen tried to inhale—

and silence swallowed the attempt.

It wasn't an attack.

It was erasure by stillness.

I. Silence Shows Its Power

The Silent Kaelen stepped closer.

Each motion erased wind trails before they formed.

Kaelen staggered as memories began slipping out of his grasp—

Not vanishing.

Not stolen.

Just muted.

Muted memories.

Muted fears.

Muted hope.

This was the Wisper path without restraint:

Silence Absolute.

The Silent Kaelen whispered into his mind:

"You let truth breathe too loudly.

You trust memory too much.

You cling to identity.

Release them..."

Kaelen's knees hit the sand.

Darkness curled around his vision.

I can't breathe...

No breath.

No sound.

Not even the Seventh Wind stirred.

Stormborn Kaelen and the other divergences remained motionless; this was not their trial. They watched Kaelen quietly drown in stillness.

The Silent Kaelen knelt in front of him, touching his forehead.

"Let the wind stop, Seventh.
Let yourself become quiet.
Truth is clearest in silence."

Kaelen's heartbeat slowed.

His vision dimmed.

The world faded—

II. Something Ancient Interferes

A sound reached him.

A whisper.

But not from outside.

Inside.

From memory.

A woman's voice.

His mother's voice.

"Kaelen... breathe."

Silence cracked.

A single grain of sand rattled.

Just one.

But in the realm of Absolute Silence, even a single sound was rebellion.

The Silent Kaelen's eyes flickered.

Kaelen inhaled—barely, painfully, but undeniably.

The Seventh Wind pulsed inside him.

Not loudly.

Not violently.

A gentle, steady breath.

The first breath he ever took as a child.

Memory awakened.

Identity tightened.

The Silent Kaelen tilted his head.

"...you bring sound into silence?"

Kaelen rose shakily to his feet.

"Not sound," he said—his voice faint but present. "Truth."

II. Kaelen Breaks the Absolute

The Silent Kaelen stepped back, hands moving to form a Wisper sigil older than any clan.

Silence deepened—so dense the world vibrated under its weight.

Kaelen closed his eyes.

He didn't resist.

He didn't fight.

He *remembered*.

His mother's smile.

The warmth of her breath.

The first word she ever spoke to him.

His first cry as a newborn.

His first laugh.

His first choice.

Truth.

Not loud.

Not proud.

Not violent.

Just real.

The Seventh Wind flowed outward—soft, steady, persistent.

A memory-wind.

It touched the edges of the Silent Kaelen's void...

and the void glitched.

Absolute Silence began to fray—

its borders warping—

its stillness trembling—
its rule destabilizing.

The Silent Kaelen staggered backward.

"...no..." he whispered, voice suddenly audible, "...silence cannot be undone..."

Kaelen stepped forward, lifting a hand.

"Silence isn't the enemy," he said softly.

"But silence without truth becomes erasure."

The Seventh Wind stirred the dunes.

The world exhaled.

And silence broke like glass.

A shockwave rippled outward.

Voices returned.

Breaths resumed.

Wind roared.

The Unheard gasped.

Fang collapsed to one knee in relief.

The Silent Kaelen stared at his own hands, trembling.

"You revealed me," he whispered.

"You separated silence from death..."

He bowed his head.

"...you passed."

He drifted back into the circle of divergences.

IV. The Next Challenger Steps Forward
The ground flickered.

Space bent.

Reality twisted like a torn page.

The Fractured Kaelen appeared behind Kaelen without taking a step.

And in front of him.

And to his left.

And emerging out of his shadow.

He smiled with a dozen faces.

"Your next lesson," he said,

"is how to fight someone who has never been whole."

Kaelen exhaled.

"Zephyr..."

The Fractured Kaelen grinned wider.

"No."

He shattered into fifty flickers.

"I am every direction you never chose."

6 "THE THIRD CLASH
FRACTURE VS. FOCUS"

The Fractured Kaelen broke into existence like shattered glass given movement.

Fifty flickers of him darted across the dunes—
some ahead of Kaelen,
some behind him,
some standing where he *would* be in the next breath,
some occupying places he'd never choose to stand.

A living contradiction.
A storm of broken decisions.

The Unheard shielded his eyes.

"Kaelen—don't track him. You'll overload your senses!"

Stormbreaker Fang shouted, lightning sparking in panic:

"He's moving faster than Zephyr. Faster than—than *intent!*"

The Fractured Kaelen laughed—not from one place but dozens.

"Why be one person," he asked, "when you can be every possible version of yourself all at once?"

Kaelen steadied his breath.

"Because that's not identity."

Suddenly the world splintered—
Kaelen saw six Fractured Kaelens sprint toward him in synchronized arcs, each representing a choice he didn't remember making.

The fracture whispered in every direction:

"Identity is limitation.
Choice is confinement.
You could have been infinite."

"Identity is limitation.
Choice is confinement.
You could have been infinite."

I. Fracture Attacks

A flicker struck from Kaelen's left—
he blocked, but the attacker vanished into dust.
Another struck from above—
Kaelen parried, but the body dissolved mid-hit.
Three emerged behind him.
Five in front.
Ten from his own shadow.
Every attempt to defend created *more* attackers.
Every swing birthed another fracture.
Every hesitation multiplied the possibilities.
Kaelen's mind raced—
I can't keep up.
I can't track all of them.
I can't fight someone who exists in more futures than I can see—
A fist hit him from the right.
A knee slammed him from behind.
Elbows, feet, palms—
every angle, every moment, every abandoned timeline.
He hit the sand hard.
The Fractured Kaelen stood over him—one version smirking,
another crying, another expressionless.
"You're trapped in your choices," they whispered.
"I am free from mine."
They flickered again—hundreds now, encircling him.

"Kaelen, pay attention," the Unheard whispered desperately. "He isn't fast. He's *multiple*."

Fang pointed with crackling hands:

"Every one of him is real for an instant—AND NOT REAL THE NEXT!"

Kaelen's breath faltered.

The fractures spoke in unison:

"You will drown in every version of yourself you refused to be."

II. Kaelen Realizes the Trap

Kaelen inhaled—

but every breath split into dozen interpretations.

His left breath tried to rise.

His right breath scattered.

His center breath trembled.

Divisio cracked inside him—overwhelmed.

The Fractured Kaelen grinned.

"You cannot separate truth from lie if there are no truths. No lies.

Only possibilities you aren't strong enough to distinguish."

The fractures rushed in.

Kaelen's pupils dilated—

And then something strange happened.

The world slowed.

Not because the fractures stopped.

Not because he froze time.

Because he *stopped following every version of himself*.

Kaelen whispered:

"No."

He closed his eyes.

Fractured Kaelen halted mid-strike, startled.

Kaelen steadied his breath.

"I won't chase possibilities," he murmured.
"I won't chase futures."
The Seventh Wind responded—gentle, grounded.
"I choose one."
III. Kaelen Finds Focus
Kaelen exhaled—
—and a single line of wind flowed from him.
Not wide.
Not powerful.
Precise.
The fractures stumbled as wind parted them.
Each flicker twisted, warped, destabilizing.
Kaelen whispered:
"Identity is not limitation.
Identity is direction."
He opened his eyes.
Only one Fractured Kaelen stood before him now—
the "anchor,"
the core divergence holding the others together.
Kaelen pointed at him.
"You're terrified of one thing."
The fractured version froze.
"What...?"
Kaelen stepped forward, wind steady around him.
"You're terrified of choosing."
Silent horror spread across the fractured face.
Kaelen touched the center of his chest.
"I choose who I am."
A burst of focused wind radiated outward—
Not violent.
Not explosive.
Intentional.

Every flicker froze—

shivered—

and collapsed like photographs burning from the edges inward.

The Fractured Kaelen screamed as the infinite versions collapsed into one—

Then fell to his knees, clutching his chest.

"You reduced me...

to one path..."

Kaelen knelt with him.

"No," he said softly.

"I refined you."

The fractured version trembled, tears sliding down a face Kaelen recognized.

"You passed," he whispered.

"You accepted what I never could."

He stepped back into the circle of divergences—

whole for the first time.

IV. Breathless Kaelen Descends

The air thinned.

Wind lost shape.

Light distorted.

A figure floated down—Kaelen without flesh, without form, without anchor.

Wind wearing a suggestion of human outline.

The Breathless Kaelen, the one who rejected his mother's gift of a body.

He drifted above the sand like a dream trying to stay awake.

His voice echoed through Kaelen's bones:

"Now face the version of yourself...

who does not need to breathe."

The Unheard stepped back, visibly afraid.

Stormbreaker Fang swallowed hard.

Kaelen braced himself.

Because the next clash wasn't physical.
It was existential.

7

"THE FOURTH CLASH
FORM VS. FORMLESSNESS"

The Breathless Kaelen hovered above the dunes, a humanoid outline held together only by intention. No pulse. No breath. No bones. A wind given consciousness.

His presence bent reality gently—
the kind of distortion that made warriors question whether they ever truly saw him at all.

Stormbreaker Fang whispered:

"...this one frightens me the most."

The Unheard did not speak.

He couldn't.

Silence wasn't weighing on him—
Truth was.

Breathless Kaelen descended until he floated eye-level with the real Kaelen.

His voice was layered, echoing from everywhere and nowhere:

"You cling to a body that was not meant for you."

Kaelen steadied his stance.

"It's still mine."

"Is it?" Breathless whispered.

"Your vessel was a dead child.

Your breath was not meant for flesh.

You walk in a skin borrowed from destiny."

Kaelen tightened his fists.

"That body is what let me protect the clans."

"That body is what slows you," the Breathless replied.

"That body chains you to identity.

To suffering.

To fear."

A gentle ripple fluttered across Breathless Kaelen's form.

He extended a hand—shifting like smoke, glowing like memory.

"Release it," he murmured.

"Become what you were meant to be—wind without limit."

Kaelen exhaled sharply.

"I'm not abandoning what my mother gave me."

Breathless Kaelen's form pulsed—like a ripple of disappointment.

"She gave you a cage."

I. The Battle of Presence

The Breathless Kaelen dissolved—

Not vanished.

Not flickered.

He became invisible wind.

Kaelen stepped back, senses flaring.

A whisper brushed his neck.

"One breath is enough to kill you."

A wind-lash sliced the sand a hand's breadth from his shoulder.

Another whisper behind him:

"You fight with limbs. I fight with being."

A strike hit Kaelen's ribs—

not from a fist, but from pressure itself.

Kaelen gasped.

Breathless Kaelen materialized briefly—

no face, no edges, only implication.

"You rely on anchors," he said.

"I am beyond anchors."

The wind around Kaelen tightened like a noose—

not choking him, but *unraveling* him.

His fingers tingled.

His arms wavered.

His outline flickered.

Stormborn Kaelen shouted:

"He's stripping your cohesion! HOLD YOUR BREATH!"

Kaelen tried—

—but the Breathless Kaelen whispered:

"You cannot hold what is borrowed."

Kaelen's form trembled violently.

His edges blurred.

His feet dissolved into wind up to the ankles.

He was losing physical shape.

Fast.

II. Kaelen's Identity Begins to Unravel

Kaelen tried to anchor himself with memory—

—but memories drifted like loose pages in a storm.

The Unheard shouted, voice breaking:

"KAELEN—FORM IS NOT YOUR LIMITATION!"

Breathless Kaelen tilted in amusement.

"Your friend lies.

Form is the Lie.

Wind is the Truth."

Kaelen's chest flickered, ribs phasing in and out between visibility and pure wind.

Pain stabbed through him—

not from injury,

but from *contradiction*.

His wind wanted to leave the flesh.

His flesh wanted to hold the wind.

He was splitting.

Breathless Kaelen drifted closer, touching Kaelen's dissolving shoulder.

"Let go," he whispered.

"Become infinite."

The wind around Kaelen swelled.

His body wavered like a dying flame.

He staggered—

—and nearly disappeared entirely.

Stormbreaker Fang turned away, unable to watch.

The Unheard whispered, trembling.

"Kaelen... choose."

II. Kaelen Chooses the One Thing Breathless Kaelen Cannot Understand

Kaelen's body flickered.

Wind.

Flesh.

Wind.

Nothing.

Flesh.

Wind—

He forced a breath.

A real one.

Rough.

Uneven.

Human.

The Breathless Kaelen recoiled, confused.

"Why...?"

"Why cling to limitation?"

"Why remain small?"

Kaelen's voice shook.

"Because existence without form is survival..."

His eyes locked with the Breathless Kaelen.

"...but existence *with* form is meaning."

Breathless froze.

Kaelen continued:

"Wind alone cannot love.

Wind alone cannot hold a memory.

Wind alone cannot protect anyone."

The Breathless Kaelen wavered like a flame in disbelief.

"Flesh is pain."

Kaelen nodded.

"Yes. And courage."

His form stabilized—

muscles, skin, breath snapping back into place.

Breathless Kaelen's outline flickered like torn cloth in a gale.

"You choose... suffering?"

Kaelen stepped closer.

"I choose purpose."

With a single deliberate breath, Kaelen exhaled the Seventh
Wind:

Not powerful.

Not violent.

Rooted.

Wind—

committed to form.

Breathless Kaelen screamed—not in agony, but in realization.

His form collapsed inward, compressed into a single coherent
outline—

for the first time gaining the thing he rejected:

Shape.

He fell to his knees, glowing faintly, clutching a chest he no
longer had but suddenly understood.

"I... never knew..."

His voice trembled.

"...why she gave us a body."

Kaelen touched his forehead gently.

"She wanted us to live.

Not just exist."

Breathless Kaelen bowed his head.
"You have already surpassed me."
He drifted back to the circle—
a little more solid
and infinitely more humbled.

IV. The Next Challenger Emerges

A pale wind swept across the dunes.
The air chilled.
Reality thinned—
Architect's Kaelen stepped forward.
Not corrupted.
Not chaotic.

Purpose incarnate.

His eyes glowed the pale light of the Hollow.
"You have survived power.
You have survived silence.
You have survived formlessness."
He raised a hand.
The sand beneath him dissolved into fine dust.
"Now survive inevitability."
Kaelen stared back at him.
"You're the version of me who said yes."
Architect's Kaelen smiled.
"And you will wish you had."

8 "THE FIFTH CLASH PURPOSE VS. WILL"

Architect's Kaelen stepped forward with unnerving calm.
No lightning.
No fractured echoes.
No formless wind.
Just purpose—
pure, unwavering, absolute.
The sand beneath him turned to pale dust with each step, as though reality recoiled from his alignment with the Hollow.
Stormbreaker Fang raised his spear instinctively.
The Unheard whispered:
"This one...
this one is the most dangerous. He won without a battle. He *agreed*."
Architect's Kaelen smiled at Kaelen.
"I am the version of you who accepted truth."
Kaelen narrowed his eyes.
"What truth?"
Architect's Kaelen spread his hands.
"That the world cannot survive freedom."

I. Architect Kaelen Defines Purpose

Wind stilled—
not from silence,
but from *expectation*.
Architect's Kaelen spoke with perfect clarity:

"Choice is chaos.
Identity is chaos.
Breath is chaos."

He pointed at the leftover fractures in the dunes.

"Every war the clans fought began with someone choosing wrongly."

He gestured at the sky where the Hollow Wind pulsed faintly.

"The Architect offers order.
Harmony.
A world without suffering."

Kaelen clenched his fists.

"A world without will."

Architect's Kaelen nodded.

"Yes.
That is how suffering ends."

Kaelen stepped forward.

"I won't let you take free will from the clans."

Architect's Kaelen's eyes softened with something like pity.

"You misunderstand.
Free will is the burden keeping your world on the edge of extinction."

He raised one hand.

A ripple of pale wind drifted outward—
not destructive,
not violent...

Revealing truth.

Sirocco warriors killing their own out of paranoia.
Mistral elders plotting forbidden rituals.
Zephyr splinter groups debating assassination.
Tempestborn sharpening weapons against Kaelen.
Wisper agents recording every breath for leverage.

Every betrayal, every fear, every deception—
Seen at once.

Kaelen staggered.

"You're showing me their worst moments."

Architect's Kaelen shook his head gently.

"No.

I am showing you their nature."

II. The Clash Begins

Architect's Kaelen moved—

Not fast.

Not loud.

Precisely.

He touched two fingers to the air.

The dunes vanished beneath Kaelen's feet—

not as destruction,

but as *restructuring*.

Kaelen fell—

straight into a loop of pale wind that forced him to relive a memory.

His mother at the Thinker's Abyss.

Her empty womb.

Her desperate choice.

Her pain.

Her hope.

He gasped—

—then the memory looped again.

Architect's Kaelen's voice echoed:

"You cling to pain that no longer serves purpose.

I remove the burden."

Kaelen forced himself upright.

"You're not removing pain.

You're removing meaning."

He swung his arm—Divisio flaring—

But Architect's Kaelen touched the counter-breath instantly, neutralizing it.

"Your second ability cannot separate truth from truth."

He stepped closer.

"You see choices as paths.

I see them as obstacles."

Kaelen grit his teeth.

"Your world isn't a world. It's a cage."

Architect's Kaelen's expression sharpened.

"Cages keep the innocent alive."

III. Architect Kaelen Attempts Conversion

He extended his palm.

Pale wind spiraled from his fingertips, coiling around Kaelen's wrist like gentle vines of light.

"Join me," he whispered.

"End the suffering.

End the war.

End the burden of identity itself."

Kaelen felt the pale wind slipping into his breath—

Warm.

Comforting.

Soothing.

It dulled fear.

Erased doubt.

Made the world feel easier.

Made purpose feel simple.

For a moment...

Kaelen nearly let go.

Architect's Kaelen smiled.

"Yes.

You understand.

Choice is weight.

Purpose is freedom."

Kaelen's breath trembled.

The pale wind pressed deeper.

The world quieted—

IV. Kaelen Remembers What Architect's Kaelen Cannot

A voice echoed faintly.

Not divine.

Not mythic.

Personal.

His mother's voice.

Saying his name.

Not as a command.

Not as destiny.

As love.

Kaelen's eyes snapped open.

He whispered:

"I choose."

Architect's Kaelen nodded eagerly.

"Yes. Choose purpose—"

Kaelen pulled his arm free, exploding the pale wind binding him.

"No."

His voice shook the dunes.

"I choose struggle.

I choose effort.

I choose the right to fail.

I choose the right to grow.

I choose the burden that makes identity real."

The sands surged around him as the Seventh Wind ignited.

Architect's Kaelen stepped back—

the first sign of uncertainty he had shown.

"You reject perfection?"

Kaelen raised his hand.

"I reject a world without choice."

V. Kaelen Turns Purpose Against Purpose

He inhaled—
And Divisio awakened.
Not separating truth from lie...
But separating **purpose** from **control**.
Pale wind cracked.
The Architect's influence trembled.
Architect's Kaelen recoiled, shocked.
"You cannot separate those—"
Kaelen stepped forward.
"I just did."
The pale wind shattered around him like broken glass.
Architect's Kaelen staggered, clutching his chest—
as though something precious had been ripped from him.
"Without control," he gasped,
"What is purpose?"
Kaelen answered softly:
"Purpose without control... is compassion."
Architect's Kaelen froze.
His pale wind dimmed.
His eyes softened—not with arrogance, but with understand-
ing he desperately didn't want.
"You've evolved beyond me," he whispered.
He stepped back into the circle, gaze lowered.
"You passed.
You remain yourself."

VI. The Final Divergence Steps Forward

The dunes darkened.
Shadows sharpened.
Light thinned.
Sound sank.
The Void Kaelen drifted forward—
Not walking.
Not floating.

Existing.

A hollow outline shaped like Kaelen, filled with a depth that should not exist.

Every other divergence backed away.

Even Architect's Kaelen trembled.

The Void Kaelen's voice was a cold wound in the world:

"You have defeated strength.

You have defeated silence.

You have defeated freedom from form.

You have defeated purpose."

He lifted his empty, shapeless hand.

The dunes turned black and crumbled into dust.

"Now face the Kaelen...

who chose nothing."

Kaelen inhaled sharply.

Because this wasn't a test of memory.

Or identity.

Or evolution.

This was a test of existence itself.

9   "THE FINAL CLASH — VOID VS. BEING"

The Void Kaelen stepped forward.

Not a silhouette.

Not a shadow.

Not formless wind.

A **hollow absence** shaped like Kaelen, outlined only so the world could remember where *not* to look.

The sand around him didn't move—

it simply ceased to exist where his feet should have touched it.

Stormbreaker Fang stumbled back, thunder rattling out of rhythm.

"Kaelen—this one isn't wind. He's—he's NOT wind!"

The Unheard whispered, eyes widening to a terror even he had never felt:

"He is unbeing. A choice that never became breath."

The Void Kaelen turned his head toward the real Kaelen.

Reality dipped—

a slight, nauseating tilt

as if existence reconsidered itself.

His voice was a negative imprint of sound:

"You fight for identity."

Kaelen steadied his breath.

"Yes."

"You fight for memory."

"Yes."

"You fight for choice."

"Yes."

The Void Kaelen leaned slightly forward.

"Then you fight for suffering."

Wind died.

Light wilted.

Every other divergence vanished from visibility, forced back by the Void's presence.

Kaelen alone remained standing in a shrinking world of pale emptiness.

I. Void Kaelen Defines Nothingness

The Void Kaelen extended an empty hand.

Not palm.

Not fingers.

Just outline.

"Everything you cling to breaks."

Sand evaporated beside him.

"Everything you protect dies."

Two dunes collapsed into blank space.

"Every choice ends in regret."

Kaelen felt his heartbeat stutter.

"Every truth ends in conflict."

Wind behind him inverted—

as if trying to escape creation itself.

The Void Kaelen's hollow eyes glowed softly.

**"So I chose nothing.
And nothing chose me."**

Kaelen whispered:

"You're the Kaelen who refused to exist..."

Void Kaelen corrected him:

"I am the Kaelen who refused to matter."

II. The Attack That Isn't an Attack

Void Kaelen didn't move.

He didn't strike.

He didn't project wind or pressure.

He simply **removed** the space between them.

Kaelen stumbled forward—not pushed, but *pulled* into absence.

His foot touched a patch of sand—

—and the sand vanished.

A wave of disorientation shot up his spine.

His sense of self flickered.

He felt—

...lighter?

...thinner?

...unanchored?

Kaelen gasped.

"What—what did you take?"

Void Kaelen tilted his hollow head.

"The part of you that needed to know."

Kaelen staggered.

His fear didn't increase—

it simply disappeared.

Not conquered.

Not accepted.

Removed.

Kaelen clutched his chest.

"I can't feel—my instincts—my warnings—my—"

Void Kaelen stepped closer.

**"Conflict makes you hesitate.
Fear makes you cling to identity.
Instinct makes you react.
I relieve you of all three."**

Kaelen dropped to one knee.

The Seventh Wind dimmed into a thin flicker around him.

Stormborn Kaelen shouted from the sidelines:

"KAELEN! HOLD ON TO SOMETHING—ANYTHING!"

The Void Kaelen turned slightly.

Thunder died mid-crash.
Lightning froze mid-air.
Stormborn's voice muted.
Only Kaelen remained.
Void Kaelen whispered:
"You are almost free."

II. Kaelen Faces Oblivion

Kaelen tried to breathe—
but breath came out thin, fragile, meaningless.
He tried to stand—
but the concept of standing felt unimportant.
He tried to remember—
but every memory slid out of reach like water through fingers.
His mother.
The Unheard.
The clans.
The winds.
Himself.
All drifting into painless, peaceful nothing.
Void Kaelen knelt in front of him.
**"Let go of being.
Let go of burden.
Let go of self."**
Kaelen's vision dimmed.
Color drained.
Edges blurred.
His outline flickered.
Void Kaelen placed an empty hand where Kaelen's heart should be.
"You were never meant to exist."
Kaelen whispered, fading:
"...maybe..."

His body dissolved to the waist.

Void Kaelen's hollow voice softened.

"Yes.

Come home."

Kaelen's hands blurred away into nothing.

His breath flickered

IV. Kaelen Finds the One Anchor Void Cannot Touch

—but something flickered deeper.

Not memory.

Not fear.

Not identity.

Choice.

Not the idea.

The act.

The decision that made him Kaelen.

The decision that separated him from this void-born version.

The decision that entered the Hollow.

The decision that saved the clans.

The decision that made him fight when everything said he couldn't.

Kaelen whispered:

"...I choose..."

Void Kaelen froze.

"What?"

Kaelen's voice sharpened.

Louder.

Clearer.

"I choose to exist."

The Seventh Wind ignited inside him—

weak

wounded

but undeniable.

Kaelen's legs reformed.

His hands returned.

His breath took shape.

Void Kaelen stumbled backward—shocked.

"No one chooses existence when nothingness is offered…"

Kaelen stood fully, wind swirling around him like reborn flame.

"I do."

He pointed at the Void.

"I exist because I choose to."

V. Kaelen Turns Void Against Itself

Kaelen inhaled—

And Divisio awakened for the third time.

Not separating truth from lie.

Not separating purpose from control.

Separating **existence** from **absence**.

The air cracked.

Void Kaelen screamed—not in volume, but in distortion.

His outline flickered violently.

His hollow center spasmed.

Kaelen stepped forward.

"You're not the absence of meaning."

Another step.

"You're the absence of choice."

Void Kaelen recoiled in horror.

Kaelen's final breath burst outward—

A declaration.

A claim.

A reality.

"And I choose life."

Void Kaelen shattered—

Not into dust or wind
but into **possibility**.

He dissolved into six drifting fragments of negative breath, all whispering the same final words:

"...choice... is stronger than nothing..."

Then he faded into harmless shadow.

VI. The Convergence Ends

Kaelen fell to one knee, breath ragged, identity trembling but intact.

The six divergences stepped into a line before him.

Stormborn bowed.

Silent lowered his head.

Fractured stood whole for the first time.

Breathless glowed faintly with new understanding.

Architect's Kaelen placed a hand on his chest in respect.

Void did not return—its choice completed.

Stormborn spoke for them all:

"You have surpassed every path you could have become."

The Unheard trembled with awe.

Stormbreaker Fang stepped forward, stunned.

Kaelen rose slowly.

Stormborn finished:

"Now the winds will follow the one Kaelen who chose himself."

The dunes shook.

The sky rippled.

The fracture glowed—

Because the Hollow Wind had witnessed everything.

And now?

Now it had formed its own conclusion.

1⁰ "THE HOLLOW DECISION"

Location: The Barrens
Immediately Following the Sixth Convergence

The fracture pulsed.
Once.
Twice.
Then the dunes went silent.
Not wind-silence.
Not Wisper-silence.
A deeper, cosmic quiet—
a silence that meant *something was deciding.*
The Unheard stepped beside Kaelen, shadows trembling.
"It watched everything," he whispered.
Stormbreaker Fang tightened his grip on his spear.
"Did we pass some kind of—trial?"
"No," the Unheard murmured.
"He passed. We didn't."
Kaelen didn't move.
His breath was thin.
His body was exhausted.
His wind flickered.
But his eyes stayed fixed on the fracture.
Because something inside it was breathing.
The Hollow Wind.
Breathing Kaelen in.
Studying him.
Choosing him.

The fracture widened—

just enough to reveal a silhouette made of nothing, framed by pale light.

A voice unfurled—

Not the shadow.

Not the echo.

Not any divergence.

This was the Hollow Wind **itself** speaking.

A voice older than storms,

older than breath,

older than the winds that shaped the world.

I. The Eighth Wind Speaks an Oath

"...Seventh Wind..."

Kaelen's lungs tightened.

Stormborn fell to one knee instinctively.

Zephyr flickers in the distance collapsed under the pressure.

Sirocco heat died instantly.

Mistral frost melted.

Black Wisper shadows withdrew like frightened children.

Only Kaelen remained standing.

Barely.

The voice deepened:

"...you have chosen being..."

Kaelen swallowed.

"Yes."

"...you have chosen memory..."

"Yes."

"...you have chosen limitation, truth, burden, struggle, and pain..."

His voice steadied.

"Yes."

The fracture trembled—

As though the Hollow Wind were inhaling the truth he had spoken.

Then:

"...and by choosing them... you have become the threat I feared most."

Stormbreaker Fang's eyes widened.

"WHAT?"

The Unheard whispered hoarsely:

"Oh no..."

II. The Hollow Wind Explains the Real Truth

The Hollow Wind stepped closer to the tear—

not entering,

not fully revealing itself,

but showing the outline of its intention.

"...I do not devour for hunger...

I devour for balance..."

Kaelen frowned.

"Balance? You are erasing the world!"

The Hollow Wind pulsed.

"...because your world is broken..."

Lightning cracked across the sky.

The sands buckled beneath their feet.

The fracture glowed with unbearable truth.

"...identity has spiraled out of control...

breath has forgotten its purpose...

choice has become chaos..."

Its voice sharpened.

"...and you, Seventh Wind, have proven that one identity can resist all correction."

Kaelen froze.

Suddenly he understood:

The Hollow Wind wasn't trying to kill him.

It was trying to **prevent him**.

Prevent what?

Stormborn whispered:

"The Hollow believes Kaelen's evolution will break the world…"

The Hollow Wind confirmed:

"…you unify winds never meant to be united…

you discover truths never meant to be revealed…

you evolve beyond the bounds that protect existence…"

A deeper silence followed.

Then the Hollow Wind delivered the verdict:

"…you are the future that must be stopped."

Kaelen's heartbeat slammed in his ears.

He whispered:

"I'm… the enemy?"

The Hollow Wind answered gently—

"…you are the axis on which all outcomes turn. And so…

you will be the one I erase first."

The world *lurched*.

Thunder rolled in reverse.

The fracture widened—

Not upward,

not downward,

but outward—

a horizontal tear ripping across the barrens.

Every clan across the plateau felt it.

The Hollow Wind's full-entry had begun.

III. But Something Unexpected Happens

The Hollow Wind reached forward—

A limb of pale unbreath forming out of impossible geometry—

—to seize Kaelen.

Kaelen braced himself.

He wasn't ready.

He couldn't win.

He was barely standing.

Stormbreaker Fang charged.

"YOU WILL NOT TAKE HIM!"

Lightning clashed with pale wind—

and turned to dust instantly.

Mistral frost struck—

and evaporated.

Zephyr flickers attacked—

and vanished mid-step.

Black Wisper shadows tried to cloak Kaelen—

and were erased like chalk under rain.

The limb reached Kaelen—

Kaelen shut his eyes—

And then—

Something stopped it.

A hand.

A human hand.

Soft.

Warm.

Familiar.

It held back the limb of erasure with impossible force.

Kaelen opened his eyes.

Standing between him and the Hollow Wind—

—was his mother.

Not a memory.

Not a ghost.

Not an illusion.

A figure woven from the Remembered Wind itself, formed by Kaelen's own defiance, his own evolution.

She looked back at him, eyes filled with the truth he had for-gotten:

"You were never meant to face the Hollow alone."
The Hollow Wind recoiled in shock.
"...this is not possible..."
Kaelen's mother smiled.
"You never understood love.
That's why he will defeat you."
The Hollow Wind trembled.
"...Seventh Wind...
your evolution is accelerating beyond prediction..."
Kaelen stood tall, voice steady:
"You made your decision."
He stepped beside the figure of his mother.
"Now I make mine."

IV. The Hollow Retreats — But Leaves a Warning

The fracture thrashed violently.
The Hollow Wind hissed:
"...next time I enter...
I will not face one wind.
I will bring all eight..."
Kaelen frowned.
"Eight?"
The Hollow Wind's final whisper chilled the dunes:
"...the Ninth is waking..."
Then the fracture slammed shut.
The dunes fell silent.
Stormbreaker Fang dropped his spear.
The Unheard bowed his head.
Kaelen stared at where the fracture had closed, trembling.
His mother's wind-form touched his cheek.
"Kaelen," she whispered,
"this was only the First War."

2nd Book

...the very near future

P^{art} I

PROLOGUE
"THE NINTH BREATH"

Wind screamed across the Plateau of Convergence.

Not in warning.

Not in grief.

In confusion.

The clans gathered in uneven ranks—shaken by war, broken by mistrust, humbled by what they witnessed in the barrens. Their breaths were thin. Their eyes hollow. Even the most seasoned warriors clung to the idea that the ground beneath them still belonged to reality.

Kaelen stood at the center of the amphitheater.

His mother's wind-form—faint, flickering—hovered beside him, already beginning to fade.

The Unheard lingered to Kaelen's left, shadows wavering like frightened birds.

Stormbreaker Fang stood to his right, eyes locked on the sky, gripping Stormbreaker Fang as if expecting it to vanish.

Above them all, the Plateau was quiet.

Too quiet.

Kaelen felt the memory of the Hollow Wind's last words burning in his lungs:

"The Ninth is waking."

No one wanted to ask the question.

But someone had to.

It was Sirocco's Sovereign, her voice cracked with fatigue:

"Seventh Wind... what does it mean?
What is the Ninth?"

Kaelen inhaled slowly.

And for the first time since surviving the Hollow's judgment, he realized—

He had no answer.

Not yet.

His mother's fading wind-form whispered:

"Kaelen... listen closely.
The Ninth breath is not a wind.
It is not a shadow.
It is not a void."

Her form flickered—
a brief silhouette of the woman who carried him, who shaped him, who gave him a name.

"It is what arrives when all winds fail."

The clans stiffened.

Stormbreaker Fang's voice cracked:

"You're saying... it's worse than the Hollow?"

Her wind-form looked at Kaelen.

Only Kaelen.

"Yes."

1 "THE BREATH THAT WAS STOLEN"

The ground trembled.
Not violently—
but rhythmically.
A slow, steady pulse.
Kaelen froze.
"That's... not wind," the Unheard whispered.
It was heartbeat.
No—
not heartbeat.
Breath.
A breath the world didn't know how to interpret.
A breath that didn't belong to any clan.
A breath that didn't obey the laws of wind, storm, frost, heat,
or shadow.
A breath older than them all.
The sky shifted.
Not color—
pattern.
The clouds twisted into spirals that didn't match the rotation
of the world.
Light bent around empty space.
Shadows lengthened against the sun.
The pulse grew louder.
Thump—
Thump—
Thump—

Kaelen stepped forward, instinct screaming from every direction.

"This... is not a wind waking."

Stormbreaker Fang tightened his grip.

"Then what is it?"

Kaelen's voice shook:

"A presence."

The clans backed up.

A presence meant one thing:

Consciousness.

The pulse stopped.

Silence fell—

And a voice without breath, without wind, without identity drifted across the plateau:

"...I did not awaken to destroy..."

Kaelen's heart dropped.

The Ninth was speaking.

"...I awakened because you forced me to."

The sands rippled.

The sky bent.

The world inhaled—

A massive, ancient, unseen inhalation—

"...Seventh Wind..."

"...you have denied the Hollow's design..."

"...you have rejected the Architect's correction..."

"...you have chosen existence when oblivion was mercy..."

Kaelen whispered:

"Show yourself."

The voice responded:

"I cannot show what has not yet chosen its own shape."

Stormbreaker Fang spat a curse.

Mistral envoys backed away.

Black Wisper shadows knelt instinctively.

Kaelen felt something tighten in his chest—

not pain,

not fear,

...but recognition.

His mother's fading form whispered:

"Kaelen... this one is not born of the Primordials.
It is born of the world's confusion."

Her voice trembled.

"It is the consequence of imbalance."

The Ninth spoke again—

closer,

clearer,

as if standing right behind every living creature at once:

"I am the breath that forms when truth and lie collide."

"I am what your choices have created."

"I am the wind that is not wind."

Kaelen swallowed.

"What do you want?"

The plateau trembled.

The Ninth answered:

"I want to understand why you exist."

I. The Ninth Breath Makes Its First Demand

The sky split open for just a moment—

Not like the Hollow.

Not like a tear.

More like the world exhaled the wrong direction.

Shapes flickered in the clouds.

Not humanoid.

Not wind-shaped.

Not definable.

Possibilities.

Thousands.

Millions.

Then the voice returned:

"You will come to me, Seventh Wind."

Kaelen braced.

"Where?"

The world pulsed.

"Where breath first learned to lie."

The Unheards pupils constricted.

"No..."

Stormbreaker Fang stepped back.

"Not that place."

Kaelen's voice was barely a whisper:

"The Thinker's Abyss."

The Ninth confirmed:

"Come alone."

And then—
"Or the clans will stop breathing."
The presence vanished.
Not retreated.
Not fled.
Simply *ceased*.
Kaelen exhaled—
but the breath shook violently.
His mother's wind-form faded completely.
Her last words trembled:
"Kaelen...
the Abyss did not give you breath."
Her silhouette dissolved into shimmering air.
"It took something from you."
Kaelen's heart went cold.
The Unheard grabbed Kaelen's shoulder.
"We are going with you."
Kaelen shook his head.
"No.
If the Ninth is what I think it is...
if it was born from the world reacting to me..."
Stormbreaker Fang growled:
"You think you CAUSED this?"
Kaelen didn't answer.
He didn't have to.
Everyone felt the truth.
The Ninth Wind woke
because the Seventh Wind refused to die.
Kaelen looked toward the distant horizon—
toward the Abyss—
toward the birthplace of his breath
and the grave of his unborn twin
and the secret his mother never finished explaining.

He inhaled.

He exhaled.

Then he whispered:

"Book Two begins at the Abyss."

The Thinker's Abyss lay far beyond the clans' borders—
a wound in the world where logic bent,
where memory thinned,
where breath felt borrowed.

Kaelen traveled alone.

Not because the clans agreed—
they didn't.
They argued.
They screamed.
They demanded he let them go with him.

Even Stormbreaker Fang tried to block the path, spear planted in the sand.

"You will not walk into the Abyss alone," Fang growled. "That is not courage. That is suicide."

Kaelen shook his head.

"If the Ninth wants me alone, then bringing anyone else will kill them."

Fang's lightning faltered.

The Unheard stepped from shadow to shadow beside Kaelen, refusing to leave.

"I should be there. The Abyss distorts identity—your wind interacts with that violently—"

Kaelen placed a hand on his shoulder.

"I need you alive when I come back."

The Unheard almost argued.

Then he heard the word *when* instead of *if*.

He bowed.

Kaelen left the clans behind.

And the world gradually changed around him.

II. Approaching the Abyss

There were no landmarks—

just a horizon that refused to stay still.

Time stretched.

Then shrank.

Then repeated.

Then remembered itself.

Kaelen felt the wind thin, then thicken, then hum in ways none of the seven winds ever hummed.

The Ninth Breath was close.

The desert around the Abyss was colorless—

not drained,

but undecided.

Dunes formed, collapsed, and re-formed differently with every blink.

Tracks vanished the moment they were made.

Kaelen's own footsteps echoed forward and backward.

But he kept moving.

His mother's last warning pulsed through him:

**"The Abyss did not give you breath.
It took something from you."**

He had never understood what that meant.

Not until now.

The air shifted—

a gentle inhalation from below the world.

Kaelen froze.

He had reached the edge.

The Thinker's Abyss.

A precipice opening into a chasm that wasn't a hole in the earth—
but a hole in *understanding*.
A place where belief went to die.
A place where truths drowned quietly.
A place where destinies flattened into blank pages.
Kaelen stepped forward.
Wind did not follow him.
It refused.

II. The Abyss Speaks First

A voice drifted upward—
the same voice from the Plateau,
but deeper.
Still forming.
Still becoming.

"...Seventh Wind..."

Kaelen didn't flinch.

"Tell me what the Abyss took."

The air vibrated—
slowly, painfully, like a thought stretching itself awake after centuries.

"...I did not take..."

Kaelen frowned.

"Then what happened?"

The Abyss inhaled.

The pull was gentle—
not dangerous,
but intimate.

The Ninth answered:

"...you were never meant to be one."

Kaelen's breath stalled.

"...what?"

"...you were two."

The sand around Kaelen collapsed into spirals.

The sky deepened into indigo.

Heat and cold fused into the same sensation.

Kaelen whispered:

"I had a twin."

"...you were twin winds sharing one fate..."

Kaelen staggered.

His vision blurred.

"Where is he?"

The Abyss exhaled—

A warm, sorrowful gust rising from immeasurable depth.

"...gone..."

Kaelen's throat tightened.

"Gone where?"

"...he chose silence before breath..."

Kaelen felt something crack inside him.

His mother never told him—

because she didn't survive long enough

or because she couldn't bear to.

The Abyss continued:

"...your first breath was meant for both of you... but only you took it..."

Kaelen staggered backward.

"No... no, that can't be—"

"...the Hollow Wind sensed the imbalance you created..."

Kaelen froze.

The words repeated inside him:

"The imbalance you created."

"...the breath meant for two became the burden of one..."

Kaelen's knees hit the shifting sand.

His heart felt too heavy to lift.

"That's why the Hollow hates me…"

"…yes…"

"…why it fears me…"

"…yes…"

"…why it wants me erased."

"…yes…"

Kaelen gritted his teeth.

"Then what is the Ninth?"

The Abyss pulsed.

The sky dimmed.

Shadows stretched upward as if reaching for the clouds.

**"…I am what remains…
when a destiny is denied a second breath."**

Kaelen's blood ran cold.

"You are—"

The Ninth finished for him:

"…I am the breath your twin never took."

IV. The Birth of the Ninth

The air convulsed.

Wind screamed upward from the Abyss.

But not Seventh Wind.

Not Hollow Wind.

Not any wind Kaelen had ever known.

It was wind shaped from absence.

From *almost*.

From *should've been*.

Kaelen stepped back—

—and a shape rose out of the Abyss.

Not a person.

Not a ghost.

Not a divergence.

A breath.

A breath given shape only because Kaelen existed to reflect it.

It formed limbs as it approached.

Formed posture.

Formed outline.

Then—

Finally—

Formed a face.

Kaelen's face.

But softer.

Unscarred.

Unburdened.

Untouched by winds, prophecy, or memory.

The Ninth Breath stood before him—

his twin,

exactly as he would have been

if he had taken his first breath.

The twin inhaled for the first time in eternity.

Eyes opening.

Identity blooming.

And he smiled.

Softly.

Sadly.

Curiously.

"Brother," he whispered,

with the voice of someone meeting the world for the first time.

Kaelen couldn't breathe.

His twin continued:

"You have lived my life."

Kaelen felt tears forming—

not from pain.

Recognition.

Purpose.

Fear.

Love.

The Ninth Breath lifted a hand toward him:

"And now...

I must reclaim what you stole."

2 WAR AGAINST NOTHING
"THE BROTHER WHO SHOULD HAVE BEEN"

The Ninth Breath—Kaelen's twin who never lived—stood barefoot on the trembling edge of the Abyss.

Wind curled shyly around him, not knowing whether to embrace him or flee.

He looked at Kaelen the way someone studies their own reflection for the first time—

with awe,

with sorrow,

with unfamiliar recognition.

Kaelen forced himself to speak.

"...you're really him."

The twin nodded once.

"Your mother carried two."

His voice was gentle, unbroken by struggle or war.

"One was meant to breathe.

One was meant to witness."

Kaelen swallowed.

"I took the breath meant for you."

The twin's head tilted in a way that felt both innocent and unbearably ancient.

"No," he corrected softly.

"You *received* the breath.

I refused mine."

Kaelen froze.

"...you chose not to live?"

The Ninth stepped past the swirling sand toward him.

"I chose not to become."

The Abyss groaned beneath them, recognizing its child.

"I felt her fear," the Ninth continued.

"I felt her desperation.

She offered us life with trembling hands.

But you—"

He placed his palm over his own chest.

"—you accepted."

Kaelen felt the guilt rising, unexpected and sharp.

"You should've been born," he whispered.

"You should have lived."

The Ninth smiled sadly.

"Brother... I *did* live."

Kaelen's breath hitched.

The Ninth tapped his own forehead—Kaelen's face reflected in his.

"I lived in you.

Every choice you made, I watched.

Every burden you carried, I felt.

Every pain you endured, I shared."

He stepped closer.

"But I remained unshaped.

Unformed.

A breath without a name."

Kaelen's heart broke in slow, crushing pulses.

"You deserved a life," he whispered.

The Ninth exhaled.

A long, patient, impossible breath.

"That is why I am here."

I. A Brothers Quiet Accusation

The sky dimmed.

The wind circled warily.

The Abyss hummed beneath them like a long-forgotten lullaby.

Kaelen's twin spoke with the softness of a truth that could shatter worlds.

"You lived a life meant for two.
You grew with a strength that was meant to be shared.
You survived burdens that should have had a second soul to carry them."

His eyes—Kaelen's eyes untouched by war—glowed faintly.

"I do not blame you."

Kaelen stiffened.

"But I must correct the imbalance."

Kaelen felt the temperature drop.

Not cold.
Not heat.

A perfect neutrality—
the calm of a breath that hasn't decided what it wants the world to be.

"What does that mean?" Kaelen asked quietly.

His twin raised a hand to Kaelen's chest.

Kaelen didn't move.

"You've evolved beyond all seven winds," the Ninth whispered.
"You've surpassed every version you could have become."

His hand hovered close enough for Kaelen to feel the pull.

"And you are breaking the world."

Kaelen blinked, stunned.

"I—what?"

The Ninth's voice remained calm.

"You are too strong.
Too adaptable.
Too willing to become what should never exist."

Kaelen stepped back.

"No—wait—"

His twin stepped forward with patient inevitability.

"I am not here to kill you."

Kaelen froze.

"I am here to take back my breath."

II. The Twins Claim

Light arced between them—
not lightning,
not wind,
not Hollow pressure.

Two identities colliding.

Two destinies touching.

Kaelen's breath stuttered—
not from fear,
but from resonance.

He and his twin were mirrors.
Incompatible mirrors.

"I cannot survive without what you carry," the Ninth murmured.
"And you cannot become what the world needs...
while holding what isn't fully yours."

Kaelen felt the truth hammering inside him.

His power, his instinct, his impossible evolution
Part of it never belonged to him.

Part of it belonged to the brother who never breathed.

"Give me back what was mine," the Ninth said gently, "and we both live."

Kaelen whispered:

"And if I refuse?"

The Ninth lowered his hand.

His expression dimmed.

"Then the Hollow Wind will erase you."

Kaelen felt something inside him twist.

The Ninth continued:

"And if the Hollow does not...
I will have to."

III. The Request No Brother Should Make

The Ninth stepped back, giving Kaelen space.
"Brother... I do not want to take from you."
Kaelen's breath shook.
"But I must."
The Abyss pulsed beneath them.
Kaelen clenched his fists.
"I won't let you die just to balance the world."
The Ninth smiled faintly.
"I already died."
Silence fell.
Soft.
Painful.
Final.
Kaelen's voice broke:
"Then let me give you my breath.
All of it.
I'll—"
The Ninth placed a finger on Kaelen's lips.
"No."
His voice was a whisper of wind before first light.
"You have a path the world cannot survive without."
Kaelen's body trembled.
"You're saying... *I* can't die."
His twin nodded.
"And *I* cannot live...
unless a part of you returns to me."

IV. The Moment Everything Tilts

The wind shifted around them
changing direction mid-sway,
as though reconsidering its own existence.
Kaelen whispered:
"So this is it."
The Ninth nodded.
"A choice between us."
Kaelen closed his eyes.
His heart screamed.
His wind coiled uncertainly.
His breath felt suddenly too heavy.
He opened his eyes and asked the only question that mattered:
"What happens if I give you your breath back?"
The Ninth answered without hesitation.
"You will become less."
Kaelen stared into his brother's face—
the face he never got to know.
"And you?"
The Ninth smiled with heartbreaking gentleness.
"I will become real."

V. The Choice Begins

Kaelen looked at his hand.

The hand that carried wars.

Burden.

Memory.

Identity.

Truth.

The hand that should've had a twin.

The Ninth extended his own hand.

A mirror.

An equal.

A destiny undone.

"Choose, brother," the Ninth whispered.

The wind fell silent.

The Abyss held its breath.

The world tilted.

Kaelen inhaled

3   "THE SHARED BREATH"

Wind circled the brothers with hesitant curiosity—
as if the world itself wanted to intervene
but didn't know whose side to choose.

Kaelen stared at his twin's outstretched hand.

A perfectly steady hand.
A hand untouched by battle.
A hand that had never carried weight
because its owner had never been allowed to live.

The Ninth Breath—Kaelen's unborn brother—waited without
pressure, without threat.

"Choose," he whispered again.
Kaelen's pulse twisted painfully.
"I don't even know what part of me is yours."
The Ninth smiled gently.
"That is the beauty of being twins.
We share the same beginning."

Wind rippled across the Abyss, forming a faint pattern—
the shape of a womb's echo,
two breaths curling in parallel,
one fading,
one strengthening.

The Ninth studied the swirling pattern calmly.

"The breath your mother prayed for was enough for two," he
said softly.
"But intention... is not the same as outcome."

Kaelen's hands trembled.

"I didn't mean to take everything."
The Ninth stepped closer.
"You didn't take.
I refused to become."
Kaelen stared.
"Why? Why would you refuse life?"
The Ninth lowered his eyes for the first time—
not ashamed,
but remembering something painful.
"I sensed her fear," he said quietly.
"She carried us into a world that didn't want her.
She feared what we would face.
She feared we would suffer."
He looked directly into Kaelen's eyes.
"I rejected breath so you could carry both our futures."
Kaelen staggered as if struck.
"You sacrificed yourself—before even being born."
The Ninth nodded.
"And now the world is out of balance because of it."

I. The Cost of One Life Living Two Destinies

The Ninth raised his hand toward Kaelen's chest again.

"Your breath is too strong.

Too adaptable.

Too open."

Kaelen frowned.

"You mean... my evolution."

"Yes. Your evolution absorbed *everything*—seventh wind, reflection, identity fractures, Hollow influence... even possibilities."

The Ninth's voice sharpened with a strange mix of pride and concern.

"You evolved because you were carrying the breath meant for two."

Kaelen's wind pulsed violently inside him.

"So I'm not just the Seventh Wind's warrior..."

He looked into his brother's eyes.

"I'm a merged destiny."

The Ninth nodded.

"That is why the Hollow fears you.

Why the Architect cannot predict you.

Why even your divergences bowed to your choice."

Kaelen felt the truth settle into him like a weight he'd always carried but never recognized.

"I was never supposed to be one person."

"Correct."

Kaelen inhaled.

"And you were never supposed to be nothing."

The Ninth's expression softened in a way that hit Kaelen's heart harder than any battle.

"No," he whispered.

"I was never supposed to be nothing."

II. The First Clash Between Ideals

Kaelen took a step forward.

"If giving you your breath back weakens me—fine.

If it makes you real—better."

The Ninth's eyes brightened with gratitude.

"That is your heart speaking."

He paused.

"But your wind?

Your wind may disagree."

Kaelen frowned.

"What do you mean?"

The Ninth gestured around them.

"Your breath adapted to fill all the spaces I left behind.

If you give up too much...

you may lose more than strength."

Kaelen braced.

"What do I lose?"

The Ninth didn't answer right away.

He walked in a slow circle around Kaelen, studying him—

like a craftsman analyzing a flaw in a blade,

or a brother realizing how much pain his twin has survived.

"Your memories," the Ninth finally said.

Kaelen's breath caught.

"Some of them were stabilized by carrying more breath than you were meant to handle.

Remove that excess...

and the memories tied to it may unravel."

Kaelen whispered:
"My mother...?"
The Ninth nodded.
"You could lose the intensity of her memory.
Not forget her—
but feel her less."
Kaelen staggered backward.
Wind around him flickered in distress.
"Why wouldn't you tell me that first?" he demanded.
His brother's voice softened painfully.
"Because I wanted your choice to be honest.
Not driven by fear."
Kaelen clenched his fists.
"I would still choose you."
The Ninth whispered:
"I know.
That's what scares me."

III. The Ninth Breath Makes His First Stand

Kaelen stepped closer again.
"Take what's yours."
The Ninth inhaled sharply—
surprised, touched, conflicted.
"I can't just take it," he said quietly.
"That kills the balance.
We must share it."
"Share?"
"Yes.
A breath for both of us—
the way it was meant to be."
Wind around them twisted into two spirals—
intertwined,
inseparable,
mirroring unborn twins.

The Ninth raised both hands.

"One spiral is you.

One is me."

Kaelen reached out instinctively—

but the Ninth pulled back.

"Not yet.

You don't understand the cost."

"I already said I accept it."

The Ninth shook his head.

"There is a deeper cost."

Kaelen's jaw tightened.

"What deeper cost?"

The Ninth closed his eyes.

Then he opened them with a calm that felt like a blade pressed gently to the heart.

"If we share breath..."

He stepped forward until their foreheads almost touched.

"...our destinies merge."

Kaelen blinked.

"What does that mean?"

"It means that whatever happens to one of us— happens to both."

Kaelen froze.

"If the Hollow kills me..."

The Ninth nodded.

"...I die too."

"And if something kills you—"

The Ninth nodded again.

"...you die with me."

Kaelen stepped back, breath trembling.

"You're tying our lives together."

"I am restoring what was owed."

Kaelen swallowed.

"And what happens to the world if our destinies merge?"

The Ninth answered with quiet certainty:

"It will shake.

Every wind.

Every prophecy.

Every balance.

Because the Seventh will no longer be a single path..."

He placed his hand against Kaelen's chest.

"...but twins sharing one destiny."

IV. The Threshold of That Choice

Kaelen stared at his brother.

The brother who should have been alive.

The brother who watched him suffer.

The brother who became the Ninth Breath because the world couldn't decide what to do with the leftover destiny.

Kaelen whispered:

"If I share my breath..."

The Ninth whispered back:

"...I become real."

"And I weaken."

The Ninth nodded.

"Yes."

"And we become one destiny."

"Yes."

Kaelen inhaled.

Slow.

Steady.

Human.

He reached toward the intertwined spirals of wind.

The Abyss hummed in anticipation.

The world tilted again.

"THE FIRST BREATH SHARED"
Conclusion

The spirals of wind spun before the brothers—
two destinies, intertwined since the womb, finally meeting
without the barrier of fate between them.

Kaelen reached toward the first spiral.

His fingers trembled.

Not with fear.

With something deeper:

Recognition.

His brother—the Ninth Breath—stood beside him, steady,
patient, carrying the quiet sorrow of a life unlived.

"Are you ready?" the Ninth whispered.

Kaelen nodded.

"I've carried your breath my entire life.

If sharing it gives you life...

then it was always meant to be."

The twins placed their hands into the spirals.

Wind roared—

not like a storm,

not like a battle—

but like a world taking a breath it had held for centuries.

Identity split.

Then fused.

Then split again.

Kaelen felt pieces of his soul loosen—

not breaking,

not dying—
returning.

Memories flickered:

· his mother
· her prayer
· the warmth of her hands
· the moment her womb carried two hearts
· the moment one heartbeat dimmed
· the moment the Abyss took something she never understood

Kaelen gasped.

His brother gasped.

Wind blazed between them as their breaths connected.

And for the first time since creation carved the winds into existence—

two beings shared one destiny intentionally.

The spirals shrank.

Merged.

Folded into each other.

A third spiral appeared—

thin, delicate, trembling like a newborn star.

The Ninth whispered:

"That one will decide which of us leads the destiny we now share."

Kaelen turned sharply.

"What do you mean?"

But before the Ninth could answer—

The Abyss convulsed.

The world buckled.

A crack of Hollow wind ripped across the sky.

The twins looked up—

—and everything went white.

"THE BREATH THAT FIGHTS BACK"
Finale

Light exploded.

Kaelen hit the ground hard, sand scorching beneath him.

His brother appeared beside him—

but flickering, unstable, half-formed.

Something tore the sky open above them.

Not the Hollow Wind.

Not the Ninth Breath.

Something older.

Something outside the cycle of the Winds.

The twins stood slowly as a shape formed in the tear—

a silhouette made of *breathless light*,

a presence so immense every wind bent in involuntary submission.

Kaelen whispered:

"...that's not the Hollow..."

His brother whispered:

"...that's not the Primordials..."

The voice that followed shook the world to its bones.

"THE SHARED DESTINY IS A VIOLATION."

Kaelen staggered.

The Ninth clutched his chest.

Stormbreaker Fang—miles away—felt the shockwave and fell

to his knees.

The Unheards shadows recoiled in terror, screaming without sound.

The voice thundered again:

"TWO BEINGS MAY NOT HOLD ONE FUTURE."

Kaelen shouted back:

"We didn't break fate—fate broke *us*! He never got a chance to live!"

The sky rippled in fury.

"THEN HE WILL LIVE—

AND YOU WILL END."

The Ninth stepped in front of Kaelen, wind spiraling defensively.

"No."

His voice trembled but held.

"You will not erase him to correct a flaw that I created."

The presence spoke with cold inevitability.

"THE BROTHER WHO REFUSED BREATH IS AN ERROR.

BOTH OF YOU MUST BE RESET."

The world shook violently.

The twins braced themselves—

—but a sudden pulse of light burst from Kaelen's chest.

A symbol neither twin had ever seen burned across the sky:

∞

Infinity.

A loop without beginning or end.

A cycle unbound by the Winds.

The presence hesitated.

Not in fear—

in *confusion*.

Kaelen's body glowed with the mark.

So did his brother's.

The shared destiny—the merged breath—had created something the universe had not accounted for:

A Ninth Path.
Not destruction.
Not Hollow.
Not wind.
Not absence.
A new evolutionary breach.

The presence roared:

"THIS CANNOT EXIST."

Kaelen shouted back:

"Then learn to exist with it!"

The sky split wider—

and the presence reached for the twins.

The Ninth grabbed Kaelen's arm.

"Brother—RUN!"

Kaelen tried—

But the ground beneath them cracked open like a shattered mirror.

Reality tore.

Not into the Hollow.

Not into the Abyss.

Into a domain no wind had ever entered.

The presence whispered:

"THE TWINS WILL BE SEPARATED UNTIL ONE DESTINY REMAINS."

Kaelen screamed:

"NO DO NOT TAKE HIM!"

The Ninth reached out, fingers brushing Kaelens

And then the world consumed them.

K aelen woke in darkness.
Not void.

Not Hollow.

Not silence.

Something worse:

Aloneness.

His brother was gone.

The merged wind was torn apart.

His destiny had been severed.

And a final, impossible whisper echoed across the broken plane:

Kaelen opened his eyes.

A single line of glowing wind hovered before him:

Find me

before they do.

His twin's voice.

Alive.

Hunted.

Becoming something unimaginable.

Kaelen clenched his fists.

The war wasn't against the Hollow anymore.

It wasn't against the Winds.

It wasn't even against destiny.

It was against reality itself.

The wind screamed

Epilogue

"WHEN THE SKY SPLIT TWICE"
Recorded by no scribe.
Preserved by no clan.
Surviving only because the wind itself refused to forget.
It began with silence.
Not the calm kind.
Not the night-before-storm kind.
But a silence so absolute the world forgot that sound had ever existed.
The Plateau of Convergence shook under it.
Every clan—Sirocco, Zephyr, Tempest, Mistral, Wisper—
felt the silence crawl into their bones
as two fractures tore through the sky.
One fracture had been expected.
Feared.
Prepared for.
The second—
No prophecy had spoken of it.
No oracle had warned of it.
No wind had dreamed of it.
When the second tear opened,
the world understood its mistake:
The Architect was never singular.
The Hollow Wind was never alone.
Two pale rifts gaped across the heavens,
each humming with the same hunger—
the hunger to return creation to nothing.

Then the first Hollow Wind stepped through.

A silhouette of absent breath.

A negative shape.

A quiet that unmade sound.

A presence that devoured memory.

Then the second stepped beside it.

Sirocco's flames died in an instant.

Mistral frost cracked.

Zephyr flickers misfired.

Tempest thunder muted.

Wisper shadows recoiled.

Two Hollow Winds.

Two perfect stillnesses.

Two ends of the world.

But the clans were not the ones they had come for.

No—

they were hunting Kaelen.

The Seventh Wind.

The Threshold Wind.

The flaw the Architect wanted erased.

Kaelen stepped forward alone,

Seventh Wind coiling around him like a wounded serpent,

light trembling against the weight of approaching void.

Wind fled his body.

Breath grew shallow.

Identity frayed.

But Kaelen did not fall.

He looked up at the two Hollow Winds

and whispered a line that the winds themselves would carry into legend:

"Then come.

All of you."

The fractures pulsed in answer.

Because the Architect had heard him.

Because the Architect had been waiting.

Because Kaelen had only stalled its entrance—

not stopped it.

The Hollow Winds moved.

The clans screamed.

The world cracked.

And the Seventh Wind finally understood the truth:

This was not a war of survival.

This was a war of becoming.

The last recorded breath of the prologue ends with a single

line,

etched into the memory of the Remembered Wind itself:

"And so the Ninth Wind began to awaken."